THE EPILOGUE EVENT

Book 1 of the AI Aftermath Series

S G BELL

The Book Guild Ltd

First published in Great Britain in 2024 by
The Book Guild Ltd
Unit E2 Airfield Business Park,
Harrison Road, Market Harborough,
Leicestershire. LE16 7UL
Tel: 0116 2792299
www.bookguild.co.uk
Email: info@bookguild.co.uk
Twitter: @bookguild

Typeset in 11pt Minion Pro

Printed and bound by CPI Group (UK) Ltd, Croydon, CR0 4YY

ISBN 978 1916668 812

British Library Cataloguing in Publication Data.
A catalogue record for this book is available from the British Library.

Rachel

Acknowledgements

In my migration from academic to novelist I have made just about every mistake imaginable.

This book only exists because friends and family have not given up on me, have helped me, corrected me, encouraged me and, when needed, stopped me from doing silly things.

Thanks to so many but most importantly, Frank Beran, Charles Cutting, Rachel Furze, Megan Bradbury, and all the students on Writing Fiction: Next Steps. Special thanks to Kathy Joy, Simon Clarke, Noelia F. Lens and Steve Jones.

Part 1

Cynosure: a person or thing that is the centre of attention or admiration.

1

22 October 2010
Two months before cynosure – Langley

It had been during a lengthy period of media sampling and manuscript scanning, early on in his tenure as Director at the Outré Literary Agency, on a cold Monday afternoon, in the autumn of 2010, that Doctor Gordon Langley had been caught by the baited hook intended for him, or, as he would understand it, when he came across the greatest story of his life.

Depressed by dreary derivative scripts, he had folded his long, lean body into one of the uncomfortable designer steel frames which were elegantly dispersed around his immense office. Distractedly he searched on his computer, coasting some of the less obvious news sites. The world was in recession and the underpinnings of capitalism were subtly reforming themselves to meet the needs of the new order. Langley gloomily considered the bonfire fed by the detritus of the burning world of ruinous loans and failed financing.

Like the movement of long grass on the plain, denoting the hidden presence of the predator, Langley fantasised that he detected an unseen narrative was in play; hiding in the conflagration, something potent, original, unique was forming, maybe even more powerful than that which was being swept away.

Langley shook his head, surprised at the lapse. He detested idle thoughts.

Thrusting the musing aside he refocused his concentration, by reviewing one of the mediocre manuscripts from a wannabe author.

As he opened the PDF recommended by one of his editors, a work of fiction by some plagiarist of Orwell or Haig; Eco or Bradbury, Langley halted, mid-mouse clicks.

The manuscript with the message had been security code enabled. As he watched, it opened and the page slid, revealing text:

Langley, this is for you. Just for you.

If the editor who had processed the work had seen this, they had not mentioned it. And surely, they would. This was for his eyes only.

"Clever," Langley breathed, his curiosity peeked.

Resting his narrow chin on his open palm and scrolling down the virginly open page, he read:

The way forward for you is as you thought. Can you find that thought? We are already there. Are you coming?

Langley, long trained in mental torture of the innocent, was an old cynic. He thought he understood motivations of all kinds, and he thought he understood what this was too.

But it was amusing. As he typed an anodyne response, a 'time-to-breath' tactic, he murmured to himself,

It would seem that someone with a high degree of self-conceit wishes me to join them dans un voyage incomparable.

He read on.

Don't assume you know who, what, or why we are. But we have something you have wanted for some time. We are what you have sought for your entire life.

Langley's PA, Esther, would have been shocked to hear the director guffaw. Langley glanced up from his screen – the doorway to his office was void; no sound came from beyond. Returning to his computer with a degree of scepticism and mockery:

Are you indeed that which purports to be what I am seeking?

He grinned, a mirthless smile. But he was completely captivated.

He did not know it, but it was at this exact moment, as he leaned into the noetic algorithm associated with the viral meme held in the document on his computer, that he was mentally snared and secured for use at light speed. But the virus jump was subtle, the transition from digital to analogue, liquid. It moved imperceptibly, below the level of Langley's consciousness. He thought he was still in command of his actions. He continued to type, to probe. *Let's see how deep the rabbit burrow goes.*

Langley flattered himself as being excellent at critical reading and critical thinking. Newsworthy items, bestsellers, and public fodder were all well understood by him. He prided himself that he could detect a good, sellable story from worthy, well-written froth from the title page, and certainly by the end of the first paragraph.

But he was getting something different here. As the implications of the story that was unfolding grew in his mind, he found himself being focused, channelled. His only conscious thought was that, maybe, just maybe, this could be important.

Reading on, absorbed even as he was reeled in, he was allowed to understand more and more of the implications of the plan. A degree of belief was needed, but the credentials of the sender were impeccable.

Dr Langley, you have been ruthlessly selected from a pool of thousands. We have a power, a capacity, and you have been identified as having the necessary qualities to act as our medium, the cynosure.

Langley was a word professional, a man who had made his money, his fortune, and forged his weapon from words. But even he had to think, to remember the meaning of the archaic term. Cynosure, didn't it mean centre of attention? He was confused by this, but he understood and liked the rest. Particularly that he had been ruthlessly selected. Here was power.

He was already far too gone in his capture to understand the real meaning of the message:

"Langley, you have been carefully targeted with just the kind of bait which we know you will find irresistible. We have you now."

Langley could not see the predator, but cold, hard fangs were already fastening their grip on his mind. For now, Langley was super-charged with a torrent of information, and through it all, he thought he saw through a deliberately constructed veil. The economic recession and the mess of the world were the smoke and mirrors hiding the point of it all.

Plunging ever deeper into the trap, Langley thought, *This is not what most people see. Fools, they suffer the consequences, the company closures, the job losses and mortgage failures: these common experiences, the daily news.*

Langley despised news, he had always thought it a distraction. Now he knew it for what it was, that which stops people from true informing. He read on.

The vast majority of people do not see the great beast coming into being, stretching, and sensing in the deep waters of the chaos which it has formed to hide itself.

Langley was thrilled.

All they see is what they are intended to see, the movements of the waves.

Langley was not thinking original thoughts, from the moment of his enchantment, he ceased to be himself; he was a cypher for another purpose.

But unwitting vassal that he was, his contempt for the rest of humanity, those he considered to be slaves, remained acute and the perfect cloak for his own serfdom. Reflecting on recent events, he noted to himself, *A new black president in the USA, the crashing of Air France flight 447 killing 228. Michael Jackson's death. Some people might be attentive to the European Union's Lisbon Treaty. But that is unlikely,* he reflected. *Most people only take note of the 3D movie* Avatar, *released just in time for a 'wonderful family Christmas'. Waves, waves.*

*

7

Over the next few days Langley was to learn much more about the deep waters he was submerging in. He was told that he would soon be provided with a handler, someone inside the conspiracy selected to mentor him. So, he had not been surprised when, soon after his initial exposure, his PA told him that a Professor Mike Riordan MBE had arrived without an appointment.

"Let him in, Esther," Langley said good-naturedly.

No doubt this was his counsellor. Langley stood to welcome his guest but the man, large, silver-haired and bullish, strode into Langley's office and chose to sit, not in front of Langley's white steel and glass desk but rather in one of a pair of handsome minimalist armchairs, arranged with a good view over Holborn Viaduct and London dipping towards the River Thames. Having taken control, Riordan beckoned for Langley to join him.

Langley was piqued to be invited to sit in his own office, but the chain of command was still forming. He consoled himself with hatred for Riordan and sat as indicated.

Unsmiling, without preamble, Riordan said, "It's good to meet you, Doctor Langley."

But his tone indicated that it was nothing more than a necessary bore to meet Langley. Providing Langley with no opportunity to respond, he continued as if picking up on a conversation started long ago, "As you guess, the big understory of the recession interests very few; the powerful forces coming together far deeper down, the union of finance and information technology in what we call, what everyone will soon refer to as, Fintech. This is not of interest to the mob, the many. But dive further, Langley. Go deeper down, a long way down. What do you see?"

Not waiting for Langley, Riordan answered himself, "Some people try to imagine the future, but very few note the alarming and revolutionary developments in General Artificial Intelligence, the universal engine driving the Fintech changes. This is far below the consciousness threshold of 99.99% of the world. Christ! Most of my colleagues in my Cambridge college don't have a clue, but by 2020 they will be shaken from their dreaming. For now, realise, this has been brought to your attention by those who instruct me."

Despite himself, as Riordan told Langley what he was to do, the literary agent could not help feeling flattered by his selection for the conspiracy.

*

In the days that followed, and obeying Riordan's instructions, Langley sought and found a mosaic of hidden messages on the internet. And the messages interested him very much. Some gave cryptic guidance on the way in which he was to conduct himself, on his manner and presentment. Some offered insights into a worrying halt in human evolution. Some provided pleasing narratives around the nano-second advantages of certain trading platforms; about internet speed which literally bent time, meaning that financial decisions could be made before the events which supposedly triggered them.

It was unbelievable. Langley saw how change was happening, how wealth in new digital forms, harvested from unwitting investors by sly minds, could sustain a revolution. The knowledge he was gaining prompted and intensified his curiosity.

In his yearning, his ardent desire to be part of this inner circle, he opened himself and was more deeply caught. He was so immersed in the grandeur of his discovery, that he did not notice as he was impaled with a grappling iron, tailor-made from his desires; he was not to know, but it was the same process which had caught and retained Riordan months earlier.

Langley felt no pain. Rather, he was fascinated by the power and speed of the super-human agency, of amoral movements at huge scale. He found it sexy, alluring, enthralling, dazzling.

He pursued the lead and eventually was drawn in and down to the story, the deep within the deep. He found more minds there, like and different from Riordan's, more narratives and erupting dialogues.

Welcome, Dr Langley. We are busy. We have a task for you.

He smiled.

"I appear to be a little late for the event. The story seems to be well into its third act, the climax. I may need to race to catch up!"

He was aware that some of the themes were unusual, odd, inhuman. He was repelled and enthralled, but he persisted and became aware as his commitment to the exercise grew, and his hands typed rapid responses to probing questions, as he revealed things about himself which already appeared to be known, of understandings which he had only guessed at.

Langley knew that he was being groomed for something, allowed in, to a secret reality which was incredible.

He was penetrating a circle which had waited patiently for him, waited to welcome him, to promote him to the apex of the project, the point of the spear. He knew he was paying a price for his admission, and he knew that he was not sure what this was, but he was long past being able to stop.

Somewhere, a whisper, he heard of a secret within a secret and the name, the code for the opening, the Epilogue Event.

*

Back in his office, in the swiftly transforming world, Langley stared remotely at his own reflection in the window looking out over Holborn Viaduct in the rain. This was pretty much as close to the centre of things, of conventional power, influence, and authority as he could get. He had always sought power. If it could be said he loved anything, then he loved dominance. It was a carnal passion and he liked to find where it was and, whenever possible, draw it to himself, close and tight. Now, he knew that he was on the cusp of getting closer to a much more potent and prescient source of authority.

At his last meeting with Riordan some days earlier, the professor had made it clear that now Langley was part of the project, the invisible authority would determine the when, what, and how of events. But it wanted Langley's input immediately.

"Dr Langley," Riordan emphasised Langley's title in such a way, as if to silently promote his own degree of Professor, a mute, childish statement of superiority, "we need you as the cynosure, but it must be a subtle outlet for the meme. We can do the rest. Just make sure it is captured in your delivery."

Riordan had smiled hugely, in a voracious interpretation of friendliness.

Langley knew and understood that kind of smile. He had no real power and was running to keep up. Despite his loathing of Riordan and his hatred of being instructed, he had put his part of the project into effect as quickly as he could, quicker than he would have chosen. He was desperate to know more about the Epilogue Event but knew he would only learn more when he had proved himself.

Shortly after meeting Riordan, Langley deliberately created an accidental encounter with Dr Randall Munroe. He knew where the facile, little man watered. He 'bumped' into him, literally, enjoying the spilt coffee, and offering Munroe his large handkerchief to mop his gaudy camouflage shirt. Of course, he did not apologise. Munroe managed to stutter, "No matter, Gordon, no matter. So very good to see you."

"Ah, Munroe, I enjoyed bumping into you. You were on my mind. We really must find time to discuss your research. It will be a great addition to our outreach social sciences catalogue, in due course. I feel sure of it, I sincerely do."

But these were just words, the hook to buy Munroe's assistance. The academic had barely begun to reply before Langley moved him on again. "So, as I mentioned on the phone, do we have the dates for my little talks to your fine college of contrarians?"

Munroe was nodding, happy to be helpful, as Langley

ploughed on, "I am so looking forward to presenting my meagre and limited yet, I think you will agree, significant monologue at, what is the name of the venue? Oscars Place or something…"

Randall's forehead creased in alarm as he corrected his sponsor, "It's Oliver's Smokey Den, Gordon, OSD. Just off the Bayswater Road."

Langley didn't bother to acknowledge the correction. But the Open Mic Night dates were agreed, the 30th of November and the 22nd of December, mid-winter's day, the darkest day.

Randall is so easily manipulated, Langley thought. *The boring idiot's desperate to find a good publisher for his anodyne, obviously autobiographical manuscripts about post-Marxian betrayal.*

Langley had known exactly which buttons to press to make Munroe extend the invitations.

These were just the kinds of meetings, and Oliver's Smoky Den, just the kind of venue, that Riordan had been suggesting as ideal for the cynosure.

A discreet group of radicals, all expert in dispersal of conspiracy messaging. The event to be held in a small club, deep within the bustling anonymity of London. Such a small thing. Such a small group of people to talk to. Such an inconsequential live performance.

He did not know how, but his performance would contain the subliminal signal, and it would be caught on video, and the videos would be edited, polished, and uploaded to the web. And Langley's words would form the sequential slices of a cryptic sandwich, a connected algorithm which would constitute the trigger for data already uploaded into thousands of willing, believing human minds during the period of preparation. And the Epilogue Event would activate.

2

30 November
Langley's first gig
Twenty-two days before cynosure – Zoe

Zoe Sinclair was going out for the night with a bunch of mates, a short walk eastward into Bayswater, in wacky, wonderful London town.

The cellar club-venue was down among the small, mean hotels which plied their trade with tourists on the Queensway, the kind of tourists unwilling or unable to pay real West End prices for a bed and croissant.

"Come on, Zoe, it's cool to be late, but we need to get there before we draw our pensions!"

Zoe and Zeff, Lex and Alice, had on suitably hipster clothing to attend a gathering, an existentialist assembly, to be precise.

As they jostled down the Bayswater Road, among the tourists and tired workers, Zoe said, "I'm not even sure I like OSD."

Alice agreed, "Yeah, it's a kind of civilised mosh pit!"

They laughed. Zeff said, "Where people too intelligent and too privileged by half…"

And Lex concluded, "…Come to tell the world that, deduced by their superior understanding, they have come to the certain truth that we're all screwed."

"Oh, and, by the way, how clever they are to have noticed," added Alice, with a laugh.

This was going well. Lex continued. "Sure, it's a pretentious gathering of London wannabe-intellectuals, but they give us a reason to be cheerful. We're not like them!"

They all laughed again, incurring a beep from a motorist as they jaywalked a red light.

"I just can't stand that creep Randall Munroe," said Alice.

"Dr Munroe," Zoe corrected. "The cleavage creeper!" she added.

Alice shuddered. "Just the way his eyes fix on my chest…"

Zeff was still in high spirits.

"Yes, the venerable Munroe, lecturer and demi-god of the University of Sarbiton, and his acolytes, drawn together to…" here he put on a pompous voice and took a Napoleon-like stance, "to share and question contemporary narratives of legitimate insurgency."

They all laughed again. But, despite their hilarity and contempt for Munroe, they continued to Oliver's Smoky Den. It was usually a place of contemporary jazz and apocalyptic poetry.

When they had navigated the narrow, spiral staircase which took the public down from the dimly lit street into the crypt of the club, they found things had started. They were indeed fashionably late.

Randall Munroe stood, spotlight lit on the podium, incongruously imperial in bearing, despite his ill-fitting T-shirt, bald head, short stature, and generous girth. He was the self-styled raconteur for the evening.

Addressing a clutch of young, self-proclaimed radicals and neophytes, his voice was unnecessarily loud as he spoke into a handheld mic. Zoe and her friends found their way to the bar.

"A round of applause, folks, to poet, thinker and supermarket manager, Peter Finch. Peter, thank you."

Randall smirked at the back of a large, bearded man in an ill-fitting suit, who was making his way to the bar.

"Open Mic Night is open." Randall waited for the laughter. "Open to anyone. Even Peter and his interesting poetry." Randall lingered over the word 'interesting'. He was enjoying himself. "For myself," he continued, "I particularly liked the lines, I think I have them verbatim," and here he put on a husky voice, "*Dark light against the ocean of what I cannot be/A fragment gone, and a lost end to me.* Oh come on, Peter! Cheer up!"

Randall beamed as the audience hooted with laughter. The large man, presumably Peter, Zoe thought, had made it to the bar. She felt sorry for him, but he looked like someone accustomed to Randall's ridicule. The academic was still talking.

"Now, time to move on, maybe to something more engaging? Many of you will know that 'those who know', the intelligentsia, usually arrive at this illustrious venue to listen to a short talk or a roundtable, or even, just occasionally, a short and topical piece by your humble servant."

Cheers, some ironic, from the dark at the back of the auditorium. One thing Randall was not, was humble.

"…And then we can all move on to get properly smashed!"

More cheers, authentically enthusiastic this time. The music in OSD, which would begin once the speaking had finished, was provided by contemporary jazz, angry folk, jarring punk, or air-slicing metal, all freely donated by bands desperate for an audience of any kind.

Zeff, who was standing near to Zoe as she clutched her drink, whispered in her ear, "I prefer the music. This bit feels like a Socialist Workers meeting, but without the working classes."

Zoe nodded. The room contained a baked-in mood, but this was strictly literate, middle-class angst. That night, the group in the dark, underground watering hole had only one more speaker. Randall was finishing his introduction.

"To join our roster of eminent speakers who have honoured the stage of OSD, I introduce a good friend of mine and a man of powerfully disturbing ideas, Dr Gordon Langley."

There was sporadic and half-hearted applause as Langley, a tall man, his height emphasised as he brooded darkly over and behind the rotund shortness of Munroe, moved into centre stage.

He had thin, horizontal, slit-like glasses, with a slight blue glaze. Yellowing eyes fluttered briefly over the audience, the look coming from a pale, horse-long face of indifference.

He began: no notes, no slides, just his mid-range, rasping voice breaking over the assembled students, academics, and assorted intellectuals. His manner betrayed confidence, a man used to being heard. His words came in measured staccato, hefting to float in the doughy air.

"Thank you, Randall. Thank you for this invitation." Then, incongruously, "Hello, Bayswater!"

The silence which followed was not encouraging. Langley didn't seem to notice. Grasping the mic stand, he said: "As Randall has noted, I am Gordon Langley and, although unworthy of the task, I have a message for the world tonight."

Langley seemed to lack the energy to raise his eyes above the near distance and the sticky wooden floor, as if there was more of interest there, in the dead footprints of years, than amongst the audience of living people. The thirty or so spectators shuffled, unsure if the gig was worth the courtesy of attention.

But from some deep psychological pool, Langley held them. He stood, angular and awkward, on the small, raised podium, his dark suit apparently incapable of receiving illumination from the single spotlight provided. Statuesque and silent, there was something hypnotically disturbing about him. He gathered and silenced the room.

Zoe thought he appeared unsure of himself, or was it unsure of his message? It was as if he was not certain if it was safe to share his story.

Zeff hissed in her ear, "What a load of bollocks! Faux humility mixed with pomposity. Winning mix!"

"Yep, he just has to be one of Munroe's friends," she whispered, with a small, uncertain laugh.

Zeff, always keen for Zoe's attention and approval, put his arm around her slender waist, to draw her closer, first pulling her against his thigh, then slightly in front of him, her buttocks against his groin. He whispered ironically, "Could be a fun evening, Zo Zo."

Zoe was not totally comfortable with Zeff's attention. She knew that she turned him on; it was obvious. But the contact was not for now.

She neatly segued an unwinding move away from him, saying, "Look, someone thinks this is cool and of the mo. Peeps are filming the insect."

Zeff seemed not to notice the uncoupling as he looked to the left and, sure enough, first one then another, phones were capturing the event, presumably Munroe's followers.

Langley, supremely unaware of any reaction he might be causing, swallowed, paused, as if remembering his lines, and then, blinking like a lizard caught in unaccustomed light, continued with more confidence.

"There is a somewhat fixed reassurance held in the collective minds of those who look at the world with worry and incredulity.

"The world of depression, despair, starvation, global warming and other disasters, man-made horrors, is contained neatly in the thought: 'I can't do much about it, but at least I care.'

"And then, as if half-forgotten, the supplementary but salient assumption within the point, the feeble hope, 'At least *we* care.'"

Now, Zoe was convinced she did not want to stay. This sounded both boring and up its arse. But before she could glance to Lex and co. to see if they were ready to move on, Langley, seeming to grow in his mission for the evening, continued, more animated.

"But what if this is not true? This, the most human of responses to alarm and concern in the body social, what if this is not true? That, the reverse is the case. What if, far from 'we' caring, what if no one cares? What if, no one cares at all?"

His words were dull, unexceptional, and yet, in that dark club room, they reverberated inside Zoe's mind. And she was sure that she didn't want him inside her.

It felt like an invasion, something unclean. She wanted very much to get away, but the clicking of fingers, the accepted OSD way of showing approval, so much cooler than clapping, indicated some of the gathered existentialists liked what they were hearing. Sure, no one cared. Fuck them! Inevitably, more pocket cameras and phones were held up. Zeff twined Zoe in his arms again, firm, containing.

Langley had something about him worth recording and sharing. The tall, gaunt man had his eyes closed now, and was holding the microphone, as if he were about to sing.

A long pause, the rasping tenor voice, now heard as concussion, more a rhythm in the chest than sound to the ears.

"What if the cases of others caring for each other was actually so vanishingly small as to be noted merely as outliers of the fundamental rule? That no one gives a flying fuck."

Caught like flies in amber, the audience liked this too. Cleverness with bad language. What was there not to like?

More finger clicking of approval, a few grunts of agreement from the neo-Stalinists raising their heads, lager suds in their moustaches.

Langley was hammering on the open door of the deniers of social kindness, of wellbeing, of liberal empathy.

"Build on this, allow me the space to develop my theme. I can sense your discomfort at my stupidity. Maybe you feel that I am making a monkey of myself, making absurd and counter-intuitive statements like this. Maybe you would like me to shuffle back to my cave and get depressed by myself, leave you and your gaggle of friends to have fun, laugh and, most importantly of all, care for each other."

He wanted to provoke them. Given what he said next, Zoe was sure this was the case.

In a tone of oily melodrama, he said, "You want to send each other Christmas cards, visit in hospital, buy a consoling drink at the end of a hard day, put an arm around the sagging shoulders, and a gentle kiss on the head to indicate that, yes, today sucked. But we are there for you, friends are in place, and tomorrow will be another day. Oh please, we really, really care!"

He had the room now. Locked in the paradox of the spell.

They damn well didn't care! They understood the cruelty and emptiness of the universe. Evolution was working towards pointlessness, without any requirement for any kind of human satisfaction, happiness, whatever! People were the curse of the world.

Provoked and enthralled, the room darkened in the tension, the vortex of intense silence. Langley, almost looking down at his own feet now, a lonely, whitely lit, black verticality, a dark window into the emptiness of night.

No clicking of fingers, no grunts or rustles; the room waited, hesitant to make the wrong noise, the wrong move. They sensed the trap and none of those in the cellar had the intention of being the first to be caught. Zoe realised that she was unable to move, she was held so firmly by Zeff.

Langley relaxed a little more, just enough to show how much he was in command. Quicker now, more conversational.

"I know the old argument, probably the one that lies at the root of your dismissal of my words, that evolution does not care, but that human beings do. That is what makes us different. Yes?"

He asked the question of the room. Swiftly, he answered himself.

"Surely, every day provides us with copious and compelling evidence that people care for each other in an unconditional and, well, human way. Indeed, the only human beings who don't care about others are… what are they?" Silence. He let the moment extend again. Then, "We call them psychopaths and sociopaths."

And there it was. He had broken down a wall into something else. He had named the monster waiting to be let in. But he didn't want to peak too soon. Almost with a jolt, he backtracked.

"I never was too clear on what the difference was between psych and socio, just got the idea that they were both unphased by human suffering, that they enjoyed it. That they enjoyed… doing it."

There was something obscene about the way Langley said, 'doing it'.

There was another pause, then Langley's whispered hiss, "I find them fascinating."

Zoe shuddered. She did not want to hear more, but Zeff still held her firmly, his hands mechanically rubbing her arms, her shoulders. He was staring, apparently captivated by Langley.

The tall man had slowed his speech to a slur on the word 'fascinating'. He savoured it, the word, nearly made manifest, a sending, floating in the heavy air.

Here was the head of the swaying cobra. Langley said, "It gets me wondering."

Indeed, it did seem to get him wondering. The doctor stopped, the gaunt, silent slit of a figure, an opening to a different world coming into being, rendered to musing. The audience were held in stasis. Not even a breath could be heard now. The door was opening.

She had not noted before, but Zoe found the word 'repulsive' summed him up. How had she missed that? He was like a long, predatory insect standing on the stage, waiting for something small and weak to approach.

As if made aware of his audience as an object for his scrutiny, the doctor looked up momentarily. It seemed to her that he looked directly at her. She met his eyes and shuddered. She had been seen. She knew it.

Looking back to the floor, as if desperately searching for inspiration, he continued.

"Why are we so fascinated in exploring the mindsets of scary people, those who clearly don't give a shit? But I am distracting myself, I will go for your jugular."

Zoe felt a shake like fever. The idea of this man anywhere near her bare neck made her squirm.

"We are evolved creatures. We are of one piece with and like nature. We obscure our origins with social and cultural veneers but, beneath the crust, we roil and stagger, we seethe and ferment. We hunger and we eat. We hide this under a culturally sophisticated psychological persona of care but, in fact…"

The doctor paused, and there was a small outbreak of finger clicking as the room caught up, showed its appreciation. This was poetry.

"…we are animals."

It was the way he said the word, 'animals', from those thin lips; the word sounded primal, cruel, targeted. Again, he paused, the people in the dark room shuddering in anticipation.

"And it gets better. My thesis requires one simple reality to be accepted. That we are psychopaths."

Someone in the room shouted, "Yes!"

Langley did not seem to hear or chose not to.

He continued. "Now, it is common knowledge among psychologists that psychopaths constitute no more than four per cent of the population and, anyway, they eliminate each other, even before they eliminate the non-psychopathic.

"And I guess that would be true if psychopathy were truly a mental, antisocial personality disorder, an aberration, a minority pursuit.

"But, my dear friends…" A pause, a look which could be mistaken for sincerity, then, "…brethren. This is not the case."

Now, he looked up and held the audience in his gaze. He looked around the room, thin, yellowing eyes in those thin, metal spectacle frames; the man looked alien.

Without prompt, most of those gathered in the room stepped forward. Despite the occult call, Zoe tried to take a step back but Zeff moved her before him; she started to panic. Zeff looked so blank, so passive. There was something very wrong here. The doctor held the eyes of the audience, looking slowly around the room, now clearly the predator reviewing the available options for prey. He had made the summoning. The first point had been reached.

Turning briefly to the dark behind him. "Randall, I do thank you so much for inviting me to your group today. My fellow travellers on the byways of the unknown, from my exhaustive studies specifically in the areas of genetics and heredity, I now have conclusive proof that psychopathy is not a rare mental disorder, rather…"

Again, the pause, and, again, the audience pressed forward. The students were practically touching his legs. Langley moved his arm as if bestowing a wonderful gift upon those looking up at him. His voice lowered, almost in a whisper: "…it is a spectrum condition."

He looked down at the young people so close to him. He lifted his arm again, but now extended a long finger and pointed slowly around the room.

"You are all somewhere on the spectrum." And, almost an intonation, "You," pointing around the room with his long, thin finger, "you, are all glorious, raging, rampaging, hungering psychopaths."

Like a person approaching a fearsome danger in the dark, Zoe instantly realised that a destination had been reached; this was the main point of the mantra.

Langley had a slender, pink tongue, which he used now to moisten his lips, a film of mucus having formed around the edge of his mouth, ugly, hypnotic.

"And an element of the spectrum condition, a powerful and useful adaptation made to allow civilisation to grow and flourish, should I say, to allow psychopathic 'us' to flourish, is our self-deception that we do care. This is the perfect camouflage, so compelling it can disguise us from ourselves. You ask, 'why'?"

And indeed, some actually did, low toned, hypnotic, "Why?"

Langley did the best impersonation of a smile that he could produce.

"It is so very simple." The pause before the blow. "With conviction we can say, 'How horrible, what a terrible thing to happen!', and then to our inner predator, 'Yes, but now I will go and rest before I do it all over again.'"

Looking at the phones held high above the crowd now, directing his message into and beyond the room, his voice rising, he said, "We are wolves in the guise of sheep and all we need is a trigger, a call, a wake-up, to find our real selves, rip off our self-deceiving guise as sheep and emerge in our power, the conquering psychopath."

A shuddering wave, something close to a group orgasm, silently swept around the room. An invisible monster was moving, touching them, caressing.

The call had been heard; the group psyche was responding. Some jostled, animal-like grunts of aggression. Something quite significant had changed, and now the room felt dangerous.

After that, Zoe didn't remember a lot more about the evening. Probably those attending had originally expected Langley's address to follow along the lines of existentialist orthodoxy: suicide, and no redemption. But the talk was far from expected. A sound began to emerge from the throats of those captured: hungry, animal, guttural.

Langley had just about reached the end of his time.

Randall had been one step removed, chatting to cronies in the green room at the back while 'Langley does his thing'. Coming back into the auditorium, he noted the strange mood in the room, sensing the unease and feeling a little unsafe himself, maybe in the choppy, emotional wake which Langley was creating. Now, he was keen to move the evening on. He was mounting the stage to join the doctor, as the noise in the crypt-auditorium became louder and louder, as the audience pressed closer to Langley, mouths open, teeth shining.

Zoe had felt she was suffocating in the strange mix of vitriol and adoration ricocheting off the walls. She turned to see how Zeff and her friends were coping, and was shocked to see them now. Their faces contorted with rage, mindlessness, mouthing noises at the stage, exuding an overflowing emotion which had no name, but which terrified her.

She needed to get out, get away from Langley, get away from them all. With an effort, she shook herself free of Zeff, ducked his restraining arm and made her way as quickly as she could, back to the bar, glancing over her shoulder, concerned that Zeff might follow.

It was then that she almost bumped into the bearded man, the poet ridiculed by Randall. Close now, she could see he had a thick, straggly red-brown beard, and kind eyes, normal eyes. He seemed unaffected. His eyebrows were raised in an unspoken question.

"Are you okay? You look distressed, lady. Can I help?"

She had no answer to Peter Finch's unsaid words. She practically ran up the spiral staircase, up onto the London street. Then, gathering, breathing hard, she bought a bottle of wine at a micro market, took it home to the flat she shared with Alice, locked herself in her room, sat with her back to the door and drank steadily until she eventually slept.

*

On the morning of 1 December, the first day of winter, the day after his first performance, Langley had been absurdly proud. In his inner-city apartment, high above the banks of the Thames, he congratulated himself, as the slave takes on the pride of his dominant. Logging into his portal to the Core he typed:

"Master."

An erotic charge, his penis uncomfortably erect in his pants, he acknowledged his bondage.

"I have completed the first stage as instructed. The code is set, but I am sure you know that already. I have provided the catalyst as required."

In the digital silence which followed he was sure he detected a cyber nod of approval. He burned with pleasure to be so cryptically patted on the head.

I have been the true primer for the avalanche, he said to himself in a wave of mounting mental and physical excitement.

This was a wonderful feeling, knowing the power which now loomed, ready for release. The dominant which was waking in the prepared minds of thousands, soon to be millions.

Finally conscious of his vassal status, his spontaneous release thrilled and surprised him in equal measure.

3

30 November
Langley's first gig
Twenty-two days before cynosure – Peter

Initially, Peter Finch had been impressed by Langley's storytelling, the way he drew his audience in, chastened them, irritated them, but not too much, not enough to drive them away; always just enough to confirm their fascination with his story, a story of conspiracy, threat, and dark suggestion. It was a masterly performance. Subliminally Peter guessed that it was a kind of sorcery.

Standing by the bar, lager in hand, he had felt immune to Langley; he had been amused by the melodramatic, overacting which Langley seemed to thrive on. He was so taken by his appreciation of the craft skills, that he didn't detect the very real threat and the mounting sense of dread.

Even as the room came under Langley's control and Zoe reeled under the assault, Peter Finch didn't pick up on the sickness, the sorcerer planting the germ in his audience. It was as if Peter was in some way insusceptible to the attack. It was not until he had seen the effect on others, on the pretty girl who had left so suddenly, that he woke up.

The revelation of his resistance had shocked him into a more considered review of what had just happened. He realised that he had been noting Langley two stages removed, as if he were watching the progress of a vicious pathogen under a microscope, remote from the action, clinically safe, but fascinated by the devastating effects the virus had on all that surrounded it. Zoe's departure had brought the disease off the petri dish out into Peter's world.

Peter followed Zoe up the iron spiral stair and into the sleety wind of the West London night.

Thinking hard, *Have I just been the witness to a parlour trick or was it more significant than that?*

He was locked in the moment, unable to gauge the seriousness, like all those who live in times when terror is about to overwhelm protecting walls, about to drown the unsuspecting. Is the portent a wave or a tsunami?

Pulling up his coat collar, he said to himself, *I'm overreacting, it was just a bit of hype, melodramatic horror show. Wasn't it?*

Like many before him, his next response was predictable. Clapping his hands together and making a passer-by jump, he said aloud, "I need a bloody drink!"

So, three hours later, Peter Finch had staggered away from a favourite pub, just a few doors down from OSD, his hair ruffled and his tie askew, the alcohol blurring and contributing to fresh incoherent worries.

He was not sure who was with him. At first two or three people, and then only two.

Lurching along through the early morning streets of Notting Hill, dodging the refuse-collection lorries, collecting the piled waste bags of the night before, he slurred, "It was odd. Odd. Not just an..." now speaking with exaggerated care, "...inte-llect-ual ex-plora-tion of a dan-gerou sidea. Stupid Randall!"

"He always was a pretentious prick, Pete," someone observed.

Someone else said, "Best if we walk it, he needs the air."

A hand was in his, another on his shoulder, people guiding him past a rowdy gang travelling in the opposite direction.

Wagging his finger at his companions, he continued. "Seen pleny of those types, over the years, y'know?"

Peter stopped, brought to a halt by his delayed memory. Leaning against a shopfront he said, "No, s'not true. Langley's different. Seems to be livin the life, self-confess psychopath, an happy with th' fuckin' *Horror Show*."

He was having trouble with his eyes and still could not make out who his companions were.

"Come on, Peter, not that way. Come along. Time to go home."

A hand pulled at him, urging him. Peter stumbled on.

"If we can just keep him moving."

Peter was far from clear on one item.

"S'like he was inviting us all to a party. Party of the psychos! Ha, ha!"

He laughed, without humour, just two jolts of not-laugh.

"It's all right, Peter, not far from home now, just keep one foot in front of another."

"So, here's sa new story. A story of hate and enemy and hostility an manipul-atio-on. Langley wans to make life not worth living." Again, he paused. "An, you know wha?" Whispering now, but a sliced insight of something precious, shining, true. "He's, he's…"

But he was stumped; the sliver of light was gone.

The hand pulled him on, a male voice entreating that he walk the little way home.

But Peter had halted and could not be made to move. This was serious. He was trying to figure out what Langley was. What he represented. This was important, drunk or no.

He suddenly realised that Langley's and his, Peter's, world views could not live in the same space in any kind of peace. And Peter knew this. Drunk as he was, he realised that some kind of challenge had been thrown down to him in the OSD that night. Without any warning, a battle had begun.

The wavering strobe of mental light returned and he said, as much in surprise as in sorrow, "T' fucker's my enemy."

Something was wrong. He turned, looked down the empty road, declared to the void, "An' I don' have enemies. So, whado-I-doabouttha? Eh?"

He remembered very little of the remainder of the slow wander home, other than his companions stayed with him; he was guided and led.

He recalled fumbling with keys, someone taking them from him and a strong arm helping him over the threshold. Someone saying goodnight. A woman's voice replied, "It's okay, Steve, I'll manage him now."

And then, falling up the final flight of stairs to his bedroom, laughing with someone at his carelessness. He climbed into bed, then he was cuddling someone soft, curvy, warm breasts, hips, bum. Nice. Then, a drunk moment of almost, but not quite, lust. But nothing to do there, given the alcohol consumed over the previous five hours; that was not possible, not on that night anyway.

And then, he recalled very little more of the night, although he would long remember his dreams. And old stories from long ago, long forgotten, stories his mother had told him came seeping like a slowly rising tide into his dreams. Fantasies laced with the dragons and princesses, the trolls and the vampires of Europe of his orphaned childhood. From the dark place of his mother's departure, the unending place of sorrow, they climbed and fluttered, slithered and marched, scurried and clung. The monsters from the stories were coming back, back to the world which his mother had left, the stories of worlds within worlds, entered by the doorway of a book.

Then it changed. Now in his dream, he was a little boy again, the magic story boy of school. In grey scale, he sat next to his friend Henry Fielding. He was rubbing Henry's shoulder, comforting. Henry was portly and the other boys taunted him. Young Peter said, "Don't worry about them, Henry, I'll tell you a story, a story about magic and mending, about making the world right. Stories can make the world feel well."

Peter had lots of friends at middle school. They loved the way he spoke, wrapping their lives into tales. No matter if they were Greek myths, animal fables or, especially, the retelling of their lives but with magical twists, seemingly drawn out of the air.

"It's like magic, Peter, the way you make things right." Henry's smiling face slid away and Peter woke.

In another part of London, Zoe still slept by the door of her bedroom.

Long before the first light Peter, propped on a pillow, was staring. His arm was around a warm shoulder, a sleeping head resting on his chest, but now his mind was surprisingly clear, sober.

The wavering image of his dead mother sat at the foot of his bed but Peter knew this was no dream. Her eyes met his, looking deep within him. Following her gaze, he saw her hands in her lap; they were open, but they held no book.

"You see?" her eyes asked silently.

There was no new story to tell, because, in the great events to come, stories themselves were threatened. He could see it in her face; he knew what she had come to tell him. He knew, in some transformative manner, he knew that on the previous evening he had entered a new story and had heard, speaking from the rustling pages, the beginning of the account. Something grand and worrying had been set in motion; the beginning of a chronicle which threatened to herald the end of the world as he understood it. Bad news, but it was important for him to have it.

Peter nodded in acknowledgement to his mother as she dissolved into the air.

"Thanks, Mum," he whispered so as not to wake the sleeper.

4

1 December
Twenty-one days before cynosure –
Langley

The day after Langley's first call to the psychopaths at Oliver's Smoky Den, the director was having a telephone conversation with Riordan, alpha male to alpha male.

"My dear professor, you must realise that, even in the dreaming spires, perception is subjective. To an anxious person, the causes for anxiety are evident everywhere, within each handshake, each glance, each email, each human contact. In contrast, to the mind of, what the weak might consider to be, a callous monster, these same causes for worry make the world supine, open to exploitation and fun of all kinds."

There. He had said it. Gordon Langley rather liked his little sermon to Professor Riordan. Just to nail the point to this 'interesting' man, true, a competitor and to be eliminated, but so much more interesting than the tool, Munroe, he pointed the way forward.

"To such a callous mind, a monstrous mind if you wish, the potential for fear, its reality, legacy, all appear luridly full of promise. It is a reality tainted and ruled by what the monster mind considers to be 'enjoyment' but the neurotypicals consider to be horror."

He smiled as he said it, a thin smile which took in his stylishly empty office, his world and his opinion of his fellow human beings.

Certainly, to the mind of Dr Gordon Langley, London in 2010 looked ripe with the potential for power and the production of dread. What he, the predator's claw, saw, was not what the majority of the citizens of the busy city experienced, but that was all to change.

Riordan had organised Langley's initial contribution to the 'Great Work'. But now, following a brief and unsettling period of orientation, Langley was keen to own as much of the project as he could, to share his view, share his world, come into closer and closer union with his fellow beings, on his own terms, of course.

True to himself, he wanted to organise a takeover, with himself in charge.

From the first moment Riordan had shown the reality of the virtual, drawn the story off the screen and made contact with him, Langley knew in his depths that he had found something big, maybe the biggest thing, and that his time was coming, and, when it came, it would herald the end of days for many others. He liked this thought. It made him what he would call happy, but others, if they came close to the emotion, would equate more with the word 'hungry'.

2010 was coming to an end, and Langley knew that a global scandal was breaking.

Riordan, seeming to have all the time in the world on the other end of the telephone line, replied in a patronising tone. "All well and good, Langley. Again, you demonstrate your aptness to the task, the correctness of the decision to select you. Your first presentation has been uploaded to the internet and our evaluation shows that Epilogue Event signatures have been picked up by the docile minds as expected.

"But we need to move on to the main course. And I can now confirm that there is news, and you need to be ready for your response. The analysts here at the Foundry have confirmed the details. Treat the following information as classified white."

Langley was all attention; he was to be rewarded with knowledge.

Riordan said, "Eichmann, you know who he was?"

Langley was affronted. "Of course," he snorted, "the bureaucrat who organised the Nazis' genocide, the office boy employed to ensure mass murder at scale, but what has that got to—"

"Yes," Riordan interrupted him. "But there is more to it, Langley. Eichmann was, what some have come to realise as, an outlier for a certain mindset, the type who will say: 'I was just doing my job. It wasn't my fault. I was just doing what I was told.'"

Langley nodded, hungry for more. He could sense Riordan settling back in his chair in Cambridge or wherever the hell he was.

Riordan said, "Less well known but more importantly, others in the Reich were weaponising the mindset."

Langley was all attention. The word 'weaponised' transfixed him. Riordan could sense this and was pleased; this would be easy. He continued: "For example, during operation Barbarossa, the German invasion of Russia, before the SS troops tasked to follow behind the front and eradicate communist cells, gypsies and Jews, before the Einsatzgruppen arrived; the citizens of Latvia, Estonia, Russia, they began doing the job. Obedient to the command, some say they just got on with it. Without warning, neighbours turned on lifelong friends and neighbours and set about murdering them."

Although he could not see him, Langley sensed Riordan sitting up, getting to his point. This drew Langley forward, clutching the phone, mirroring, despite himself.

Riordan said slowly, "They killed and murdered because they were doing the job, they were operating only as cyphers for great ideas. Their susceptibility to suggestion, to accepting a dominant ruling idea, had transformed them."

Riordan chuckled humourlessly. "It is one of the thorns in global humanities' minds – how could people do this? How could people, friends, neighbours, how could they become wolf to each other?"

The rhetorical question had Langley white knuckled in anticipation. This was a deeper magic than he had imagined.

"The answer," Riordan continued, sensing Langley's eagerness and punishing him by slowing his delivery, "the answer, Langley, lies in the manipulation, extension and targeting of the Epilogue Event as code tuned to susceptible minds. Of course, with the Nazis it was an early, crude attempt, but others have explored the idea and it has proved to be surprising just how many people are susceptible. The Stanford Prison Experiment in the 1970s was very instructive. More recently academics have identified the sub rational System 1 mindset. But we have progressed much further and weaponised the entirety of doxa now."

Langley felt perplexed, didn't dare to voice his ignorance, but Riordan sensed his bafflement.

"Doxa," Riordan repeated. "The Greek word for opinion, but we can think of it as the mindset which follows suggestion. Plato knew all about it, wrote about it in his Dialogues. The doxa state is the doorway to mind altering, or mind bending, that might be a better term. Hmm, think of it maybe as weaponised brainwashing at huge scale maybe? Yes, I like that. This is what your cynosure will be all about, Langley, triggering the Epilogue Event, preparing the ground for our project."

Langley was running to keep up with the torrent of information and its implications.

Riordan, his voice purring with the power which he exercised, continued. "As you know, the first panic originates with leaks on the internet of private and confidential, high-security information."

This was a jump. Langley's mind lurched as he tried to retain his composure.

"Okay." But Langley was struggling, stung by Riordan's superiority, what did internet disclosures have to do with his brilliant cynosure?

Langley hated being given instruction or being told things which he did not already know, but one of his long-honed craft skills was a resilient capacity to store up his resentments and prepare to send them back with interest, at a later date. He liked to think of himself as above emotion and to effectively have no vulnerable pulse. For now, he contented himself with a further humble response. "Good to know, Riordan. How?"

He liked to ask short questions; it disarmed even the alpha male and drove his competitors into clear sight, revealed the kind of personality one was up against. With Riordan, he already knew, of course, but it was fun to play games.

Riordan spoke quickly now, attempting to re-establish his control. "Organised activists are leaking or, better, making public a tsunami, a flood, eventually over 250,000 classified cables and messages. The shitstorm is intense. The messages include details of strategy, the spying of officials on allies, and details of potential air strikes."

Riordan sounded happier as he described the mayhem. "It's blowing up in a spectacular fashion, Langley. The action and the response from the target is what was intended in our project. So, the waves are rocking the public consciousness, ideal for the delivery of the inflection point, the point where mass consciousness becomes malleable to, well, to our specific event horizon…"

And now, as the man swerved into jargon, Langley noted a very slight change in the tone of Riordan's voice. Most people would not have noticed, but Langley, holding the phone close to his ear, waiting to interpret every sign, heard it loud and clear.

"…Do you have everything in place? My superiors would like to know if you have any guidance or even advice on your moves over the coming weeks."

There was just a scintilla of request in the voice, and this delighted Langley. It confirmed what he had already guessed: that Riordan needed him, needed his success to ensure his own. And so, he now knew that he controlled Riordan, not the other way around, even though Riordan did not know it yet.

Happy, he contented himself with a long pause and a brief reply. "Wait." And then he'd hung up.

Riordan would have to follow Langley now.

As for the news about the leaks online. Well, the cynical abuse of power, derisory treatment of allies, and potentially war-inducing provocation, all good stuff, but there would be nothing that had not been guessed at before. The difference was that now it would be official. But this was not the real story, and Langley knew it.

Langley's profession ensured that he was an expert at recognising good stories.

His colleague, ex-co-owner of Outré and now employee, had said ruefully of Langley to a new, bright-eyed copy editor, "Oh yes, he's the man alright! He just pays us, his employees, to find the publishers and producers for authors. And we also find the poets, the playwrights, the screenplay adaptors, the 'talent' among the ocean of talentless detritus."

His young co-worker suggested, "So, we do all the unglamorous, tedious stuff?"

"Yep. He just cherry-picks the winners and prepares and ordinates the right kind of creative for the appropriately placed media. And he takes all the credit and the plaudits." A pause, not so rueful now; a tone of self-surprise and grievance. "And he's so fucking good at it. He bullied me out of my shares, and now I'm working for him! Someday someone will have to let me know how I let that happen."

It was true. Langley let the grunts do the legwork. His concern was chiefly with the gold performers, the talent who produced the printed page or show, TV, film or pod, allowing him to extract money, as if by magic, from the eager public. The production of wealth for Langley was the underlying raison d'être for Outré.

Langley was now the sole impresario of this small but discrete empire. If the discovery of profit-creating fiction was his day job, making some fictions into facts was the secret office of his ambitions, his obsession.

He walked over to the window, taking in the view, but not seeing anything. Thinking.

In his white office, so sparsely furnished and so empty of human touches as to be instantly recognisable, as being of the highest taste and the most expensive design, the phone rang again. Langley stared at it like a lizard reviewing a sapphire. It would not be Riordan again. The man knew he had 'lost' the last conversation; he would not ring back so quickly; he would just hope that Langley would fuck up, but not too badly. So, let it ring.

He continued to stare at the phone, assessing who was calling him on his most private line. He wondered if it was worth picking up. Was it a leader or a drone? The person on the other end might be anxious; they might know the large, light office in which the phone was ringing. They might know the noise it was making. They might worry about the ring going on and on. Langley smiled as he imagined the anxiety he was creating.

After thirty long seconds in that sparse, horribly fashionable room the tall man, now folded in his steel chair, picked up slowly and said, "Yes." And then, he listened.

Anyone standing behind the director, looking over his shoulder at his empty white desk on the seventh floor of the anonymous tower block, in High Holborn, just out of the way of the main high-rise craziness of London, anyone who had ghosted up behind him, would have heard nothing but his silence. Langley did not answer phones; he permitted them access. He listened intently for around five minutes, the phone held loosely in his thin fingers, inches from his prominent ears, and then he hung up.

Another tumbler had fallen, another step towards a new state of the world, a state beyond the boundaries of evolution to make a difference, a state which would be irreversible. Langley had been informed and he was becoming increasingly aware of the full nature of the powerful role he would play in the new world.

And now he understood not just what he was doing, but why he was doing it.

Whilst the early social influencers were going crazy with indignation that the only global super-power would dare to act with all the sneering expedition one might expect of the only global super-power, there was a deeper messaging going on, and Langley was one of those both receiving and, now, since his first little talk in OSD, transmitting.

There was a story behind the story.

The scandal of the leaks was evidence of the degree of access that intelligence had to machine code, and this, in turn, demonstrated the subtle outreach of a mind not human, an agency without any living pulse.

Langley shivered in delicious anticipation. Sure, the whole thing would eventually blow itself up with the distraction, the human story, the accusations of sexual assault, and the governmental spat between civilised Western nations. Rumours about bad behaviour always trumped all other forms of news. But that was the invisibility cloak, the cover to provide the mist and vapours, keeping the attention of the global audience away from the deeper story, that a machine mind could find, acquire, and transmit pretty much whatever data it wanted, from whoever it wanted, whenever it wanted. And the list of those open to easy access and expeditious extraction included the most powerful country on earth.

The invisibility of the real story, Langley's story, remained perfect.

"Coffee, Director?"

Langley had been deep in consideration of the consequences of action and the risk to himself for what would follow. The question which disturbed him was unwelcome, and had come in gentle enquiry from his PA, Esther Coleman.

Langley had told her to knock, although this antiquated concept was all but impossible to accomplish on the bafflingly modern doors of his office. He had told her that he did not like to be disturbed, did not like to be "invaded", as he put it, but she continued to do this, to courageously enter his space without warning, trying to be nice, to do her job excellently. Eyeing her malevolently from under his lids, he replied, levelly, "Good...?"

Esther, a handsome brunette in her mid-forties, her hair wound into a tight bun on top of her head, and wearing metal frame spectacles, looked like an attractive woman desperately attempting the disguise of an archetypal librarian.

She was married with three children and was a super-competent and well-intended person who had made a terrible mistake and got the wrong job, working for a terrifying boss. Now, she spent all her free time frantically trying to find an alternative employer. A library would be a dream compared to her reality. She was desperate to get away to a dull, normal job, but without antagonising Langley. In her ideal world, he would not even know she had gone.

She instantly realised that she had, yet again, made a mistake, this time in assuming that the director's open door meant that he was prepared for invasion and would allow her to offer him coffee. Her error would result in cruelties. But she was not going to compound the error and cock up again. Dutifully, she finished the phrase that was left hanging by her intimidating boss.

"Good morning, Director. I am sorry to disturb you. Would you like me to get you a coffee, or would you rather I closed your door and left you in peace?"

He did not reply, merely continued to stare at her in the same way.

Esther smiled, but inwardly shivered under that snake gaze. She retreated backwards, eyes on the floor, and silently closed the door. Somehow, she felt it was vital to face Langley at all times. You would not turn your back on a poisonous spider, a venomous thing which shared your space. She left his presence as the kowtowing, cringing subjects had left the presence of emperors centuries before. You don't turn your back on the most dangerous thing in your world.

Oh, Esther, Esther. I'm not really angry with you, Langley thought.

Turning in his chair to survey the London skyline, he mused. *Well, not particularly annoyed.*

It was just an old habit. It amused him to torture weaker things, dependent people, the needy.

Esther was worth more to him as an object for his petty cruelty than in her formal role as his PA, a role which she managed with admirable effectiveness.

But Langley only played with others as he was played with in turn.

He did not like to think back to school, the expensive private academy which his unloving parents had sent him to. Unwillingly, the image of the cricket pitch on a chilly spring morning came to mind.

"Come on, Luggy, hit the bloody ball!"

The laughter of his fellow schoolboys had been nasty. And he had remembered it.

But the young Langley had been no innocent picked on unfairly. He was victim because he was hated, because his schoolmates had identified his tendency to quiet, well-concealed acts of unkindness. Ratting, implicating, stealing, these were not the qualities to help a boy to thrive at school, or a student to gather friends at college. But ensuring that seniors knew unfounded fabrications about his competitors did assist him in squirming his way to a good job, often inflicting a certain amount of pain and humiliation following his success, rubbing in his victory.

On getting the top job at the literary agency, the lean, aristocratic, chair of the board of trustees had looked at him with some distaste and said, "Now, Dr Langley, you were up against stiff competition. Some of us had reservations about your, what shall I say, your methods, maybe? But the job is yours now, although you must realise that your position is conditional."

Langley had feigned interest in the sanctimonious bore as he prattled on.

"You must realise, Gordon, that as the director of our literary agency, you have access to the publishing houses of the world, the stories of the world, the world of communication. Furthermore, as the boss of one of the most prestigious agencies in London, you have a clear line of sight to the new narratives which will lead the thinking of our time."

Continuing in a tone which betrayed the words, even as he said them, he added, "All of us on the board are confident that you will make good use of the opportunity."

"Oh, I am so very grateful, Chair. So very pleased to have this wonderful opportunity to make my mark. Thank you all for this vote of confidence. You will all soon see the difference I can make."

And he had made a difference, including getting rid of the tiresome chair of the board.

But that was all history. Now Langley had to prepare for his main performance – the cynosure was primed; the main event would happen; and no one even knew about, let alone could hope to stop, the consequences of the Epilogue Event.

5

1 December
Twenty-one days before cynosure –
Peter

Hangovers aren't a good beginning, but he was where he was. Peter Finch had a lot of thinking to do following Langley's first performance. He'd been more upset by the distress of the pretty young girl than by Langley or his words. Zoe's anguish had cratered him deep below the surface, shifting his anxiety, an uncomfortable hollowed-out cavern of disquiet. A monster was emerging into the light. He could still taste the hops and cheap whiskey from his stupid reactive binge.

Langley had already made his way to High Holborn and his domain of glass and steel, when Peter awoke in his untidy bed to an elbow in the ribs. He had forgotten that he had company, a push on his side, the creaking of the bed, the cold of fresh air entering under the duvet as it was lifted aside, the weight on the end of the bed. Peter, befuddled by sleep, held the thought.

"Mother?"

But the voice was not the dream voice of his mother.

"You are weird, Peter, you know that? But Christ, it's cold! Jesus! Why don't you turn on your central heating?"

Another creak from overworked bed springs and the person moved off, clearly aware that the question was rhetorical.

"Is the coffee in the usual place, Pete?"

Struggling to convert consciousness into sense, Peter rolled over and grunted a reply to the affirmative. Who was it? Then, he recalled it was Becky.

Rebecca Maple was a long-standing friend of Peter and Steve's and a regular at OSD, as well as a variety of other establishments along the Queensway in West London. Despite what many of the men in the pubs and clubs around the Bayswater area might have thought, Becky was not a hooker; she was an attractive woman of colour who knew her mind. And she knew the people she wanted, as she had told Peter on numerous occasions.

"I'm good at choosing. And most men are tossers – in more ways than one."

Becky was an enterprising woman. In self-defence of the disapproval of the prurient, she was keen to argue.

"Yes, I do have a number of male and female friends, mates who I keep 'bubbling along'." She liked the term. "And, now and then, one of them might like to pay for the night out, a gift of a bit of clothing or jewellery, something 'nice'. That's what people should do."

It was a moral point, as well as a sign of reciprocity. But Becky had standards and lines in the sand. Money never arose in the conversation. As far as she was concerned, it stopped with gifts.

"That's it! I don't ever sell myself. That's not what I'm about."

God help anyone who made the wrong calculation.

When Peter had first met Becky, another drunken night at OSD, he'd had the temerity to ask her background. Becky, sensing Peter to be 'OK' but as yet untested, had said, "Originally Great Yarmouth if you have to know. Mum's still there. Small Windrush community, in a shithole of a flat. I've told her a thousand times to get out, come and join me, but she won't have it."

Despite her mother's worries, Becky flourished in London. She still looked out for her mum, a bit of money now and then, small gifts in the post.

Rebecca had a good look about her; she was, "very easy on the eye", as Pauly noted appreciatively as he poured shots at OSD. Peter loved her and counted her as his best female friend.

As Becky pulled Peter's huge dressing gown around her naked body and wandered off to find the necessary elements needed to make the first cup of coffee of the day, Peter scratched his face. His beard had squashed, a matted concertina around his face, and was in need of a good wash and comb. He needed to untangle his thoughts too.

It was Wednesday morning and, as he looked at the digital clock perched precariously on the chair by his bed, he saw swimming into crisp vision the numbers, 7.30. He still had some time to think before he needed to shower and head off to work.

Bless Becky, she had known this, she knew his timetable, and, in many ways, she took better care of him than a more conventional partner would. Peter was always happy when she was around. But then, Peter valued people; he thrived on the pure oxygen of social generosity.

But his problem was Gordon Langley; Langley was something else. Whilst he was unsure of the prompt, the sense of anxiety he had identified in Langley's presence, he knew something was wrong; the problem was he didn't know what it was.

What is it about that bloody man? he thought. *Why do I feel so anxious? And what is a ruddy psychopath?*

There it was, the core of the concern was anxiety over ignorance. He needed to find out more about psychopaths and Langley. He was ignorant and somehow knew that this gap in his understanding could be horribly exploited.

Rolling onto his back, he grabbed his phone from the chair beside his bed and looked up 'psychopath'. It was not an encouraging beginning.

There was a great deal of disagreement about the nature, origins, diagnosis, and treatment of psychopaths. The links seemed endless but, and this worried him more than other elements of his reading, there did seem to be a link between sociopathic, psychopathic, and general antisocial behaviour, people haters, and activity on the internet.

He would need to do this properly; now was not the time.

The smell of fresh coffee and buttered toast preceded Becky as she came back into the room. Peter put down his phone, smiled at her, and pulled back the duvet.

"You are the sweetest thing, Rebecca Maple."

Perching the tray and its plate of toast on the end of the bed, and bringing her cup of coffee with her, Becky handed Peter two paracetamol and a glass of water and said, "Well, you looked like you could do with some TLC, Pete. You were shit-faced last night."

Precariously juggling water, tablets and phone, Peter was also struggling with his memories, his reactions to Langley, the girl and the resulting bender. After all, he had listened to lots of objectionable women and men in his life; it was a daily hazard studying at universities with a philosophy degree, not to mention for a supermarket manager, but Langley had been different.

As she settled beside him, he gently pulled Rebecca closer and asked, "What did you think of him, Becks? Langley, I mean?"

Coffee cup held between both hands, Becky let her head rest on the pillow as she considered her answer.

"Not sure, really. He's definitely on the cunty side of things. A bit of a lizard, well, more an insect, I guess, nasty sort of bloke. Can't say I listened all that closely but, yeah, come to think of it. I was chatting to some mates, and I was surprised that they got so caught up in his little rant about psychopaths. He seemed to get under their skin."

Peter reached for, then gulped, overhot coffee, winced as it scolded his tongue and mouth, and then managed to say with difficulty, "He created a bit of a stir. He upset me, Becks. He really did. And I'm not sure why."

Becky turned and looked at him. Sad at times, yes. Mad most of the time, sure. But upset? This wasn't like Pete. Putting down her coffee cup, she stroked his head gently. She thought his hair very soft; it was like stroking a big, soft dog. She didn't like Pete getting upset. She said, "Don't let a cunt like him get you down. He was all mouth and malice.

55

Nasty. Best to forget all about him, like the rest of the world will. I don't reckon Randall will have him back."

Peter sipped with more caution now. He nodded to Becky, but could not help thinking, *I'm not sure about that. Langley created just the kind of stir Randall likes. I reckon he'll get a second gig. But why am I so worked up by it?*

Speaking, counter to his inner thoughts, he probed Becky. "You're probably right. But didn't you feel anything change while Langley was speaking? I'm sure I did. And, I remember now, there was this girl, pretty, with long, dark hair, and she left as Langley was coming to his point. She looked distressed. Other people got really angry. It wasn't normal. Not like the usual kind of talk. Am I going nuts? Did you get any of that?"

Becky continued to sip from her cup. Pete was getting worked up again. This worried her in turn. She had all kinds of ways of helping men with their worries, but maybe the best thing would be to find out more.

"Why don't we, you and I, go back to OSD when Randall is back, later in the week? He's usually about with his groupies from Thursday. Why don't we go back and find out a bit more about Langley, about what makes him tick? I bet you you'll feel a lot better for it. You'll see, he's just wind and springs. He doesn't amount to shit."

Peter felt a rush of affection for his friend. This was perfect, a trouble shared and all that.

"Just one thing, Becks, I think we ought to ask Steve to tag along. If Randall's got his gang, I'd like my own backup."

"Well, he was there for you when you needed him last night, Pete," Becky said. "He did most of the heavy lifting. He may look like a vagrant and pick fights with anyone and everyone, but he's always there when you need him. I think he's sort of in love with you."

Peter scratched his beard thoughtfully. This wasn't the conversation he was ready for at 7.30 on a workday morning with the residual of a hangover. Hurriedly he moved on.

"I'm sure I don't deserve him, Beck. Mind you, we go back a long way, me and Steve, back to uni and all the fun. In that not-at-all-cool Freudian, Marxist, Sartre, power-to-the-people, look-into-my-eyes bullshit. I blame Randall."

Becky sipped her coffee thoughtfully and said, "It's not healthy, you two still hanging around Randall. I mean, he's not charismatic or anything. Rather a charisma black hole if you ask me."

"You're right," Peter said, "but going to OSD and pretending to be young and rad, well, it's probably just the last bit of us refusing to grow up."

This seemed to get Peter thinking. Ruminatively he added, "When the time to leave uni came, Steve and I needed to pay off our student fees. I accepted the inevitable. I hadn't got a clue what I wanted to do, so I just went for the first job with a decent salary."

"Shame Steve didn't take the hint," Becky responded quickly.

"I guess." Peter said. "Steve and the system. It just doesn't work. He's always between unskilled jobs, either running the soup kitchen or standing in line. I think he has a kind of Robin Hood view of himself, a friend of the friendless!"

"And with some pretty dodgy friends too," Becky added.

Peter didn't seem to hear her; he continued, "And he's always saying how he won't take any shit from the 'fascists', from the establishment who try to 'brainwash' him with stuff like interview technique, technology training, personal improvement loans."

Becky wasn't going to let this go; she said, "Come on, Pete, he says he hates the system but doesn't seem to see any issue spending his time with drug dealers and gangsters! It's almost like he's drawn to the underworld."

Peter nodded. "But his heart's in the right place, you have to agree."

Becky was laughing now. "Do you remember that well-intended Christian type, the old lady with the twinsets, who tried to give him good advice? The look on her face when she had her kindness thrown back at her, with a lecture on the hypocrisy of pity."

"How could I forget? You know, he's definitely got to be with us for the chat with Randall. Steve can be helpful in all kinds of ways, and, OK, he knows lots of shady people, but you never know, it could be useful."

"And, as he's your lodger, you can kind of demand he come along, Pete. Let him off a week's rent or something."

Peter nodded. Letting Steve off the rent was becoming a default position but he didn't want to let Becky know.

*

While he waited for the opportunity to confront Randall, Peter spent worrisome days at the supermarket, trying to apply himself to his job with the degree of enthusiasm his boss demanded.

"Mr Finch, a moment please?"

The polite request was an order and Peter knew it.

"How can I help, Clara!"

But the bonhomie never worked. When she got him into her grey, featureless cubicle on the floor above the main store, his sour-faced line manager said, "Although you have something of a niche position in the business, you don't have license for suboptimal work allocation. You do know that?"

Know it, he didn't even understand what the words meant.

"Clara, look," he tried a sad puppy smile; if he'd owned a tail he would've wagged it, "I just organise the inventory from warehouse to shelf. I make sure that what comes out from stock makes it to our wonderful customers." He paused. Clara's face was a mask of impassive inscrutability. He tried again. "I mean I do understand." He remembered his lines from a management away day. He recited, "I'm part of the essential delivery of the retail experience, and I strive to complete my work without mishap."

But Clara didn't look mollified. Accidents occurred, and Peter had the job of HR liaison and 'talking it through' with the staff member assumed to be the problem.

"Mr Finch, the basics of the job are very straightforward, that is to make sure that the shelves are always full, providing the public with the confidence to believe that there is, was, and will ever be, plenty of everything."

When Peter had complained about the potential dishonesty, she had brushed it off as, "Necessary smoke and mirrors, Finch. But it is very important that the workforce applies itself optimally. Nothing beyond reason, just optimal. And," she cut across him as he tried to interpose, "that means being clear and concise with our co-workers and," again she spoke over him, "understanding the necessity for discipline in some cases."

Peter shook his head; the smoke and mirrors were obscuring the necessity for workplace cruelty.

He was referred on to his boss's boss, a young man apparently fresh from the management training programme. The meeting was pointless, not even about the issue of 'accidents'. Bright-eyed and apparently in love with the grocery business the young man burbled, "It's fascinating, Finch. All part of the twenty-first century mirage. It's what we like to call 'endless stuff'."

He smiled hugely at Peter, nodding his head and encouraging him to join him in wonder at the cleverness.

"We want to create a vision and it goes like this: if you have the money, you can have anything you legally want."

So, Peter added in his mind, as he twiddled his pencil, *all you needed was money. A great deal of money, ideally!*

But there had been the 'accidents'. Accidents included breakage and lost or missing inventory. It also involved identifying weak performance, talking the issue through with a member of the HR team, and then jollying along the victims of any resulting HR 'inducement' policy. Inducements were subtle, and then not so subtle: carrots and sticks for staff to improve or face discipline, which ultimately meant the sack. *Not if I have anything to do with it*, Peter thought grimly.

Many of his co-workers were immigrants and refugees, the flotsam which ended up doing the support jobs which kept the gleaming city of endless stuff running.

Filling in time sheets when staff were late, ignoring requirements for official documentation and occasionally allowing unagreed overtime, Peter was flying close to HR 'inducements' himself.

Each day, he found himself working late and working creatively, getting to bed even later, wrapped up with the lives of other little people like himself, all surviving in the great machine.

The upside was, Peter had little to no time to think about Langley until Thursday.

*

Thursday evening came and Peter and Steve had arranged to meet Becky in advance. He was so pleased she was there. If it had just been him and Steve, it would have felt like Randall having a belated tutorial with two of his worst ex-students. And he was grateful for another pair of ears to listen into the talk about Langley's monologue.

"I know I am running behind the pace of the story, Becky. I'm still not even sure I understand what it's all about. I'm sure it's why I feel so agitated."

Smiling at her, unaware that she found him endearing in his 'little-boy-lost' mode, he reached out, touched her hand.

Becky was part Peter's lover, part his organiser, and part his best friend. She did not stop to reflect that this trinity was pretty much the full set to qualify as 'partner'.

Munroe had been delighted by the splash that the evening had made. His students had alerted him to the minor internet sensation which Langley had caused, the proliferation of online op-eds on social media, the squalls and mini storms, the pervasive intensity of comments.

But, after all, all publicity is good, he thought to himself, too busy being slightly related to an infamous event to worry about the nature and future of the fame he was attracting. He was more than content to have been, to the satisfaction of his own conceit, the guiding mind behind the commotion that followed Langley. Randall was, at that time, totally unaware that he was a blind man following a slave.

He was very pleased to see Becky, whom, Peter could see, he clearly fancied and insisted on calling 'Rebecca' with an emphasis on the 'b', almost spitting the consonant and making Becky jump slightly.

It was early evening when the three trooped in and arranged themselves on tall stools by the bar. Randall was already there, his followers sat around a table some way off. Peter placed himself between Randall and Becky, providing a physical barrier between Becky and the roving, approving gaze of Munroe. Steve sat, slightly removed on the other side of Becky.

Pushing his tall lager glass away and nodding to Pauly for a refill, on Peter's tab, Randall carried on in conceited and worldly terms, following Peter's line of questioning.

"What can I say in lay terms? I mean, Gordon is fascinated by psychopathy and it's such a wide field, Peter. I mean, no one really agrees quite what it is or where it comes from. Nature or nurture? Environmentally decided or a product of genetics? All kinds of arguments are permitted and indeed have a following. I am just interested in the ideas and providing a forum. That's all that matters to me."

Peter could not help smiling grimly to himself as the self-important little man tried to own Langley and his event, whilst distancing himself from any moral responsibility for any unhappy consequences. He had just presented the blue touch paper. Guiltless crime, but not without victims.

Randall, seeking Becky's eye around the intervening bulk of Peter, went on.

"And as for the furore which has followed, Rebecca. Well, the internet is an evolving cultural context for group development, and I have been as amazed as anyone else at what has followed."

As if suddenly realising the part he had played, Randall said, "I should note, and I'm sure you will follow me on this, no one is saying that the internet creates psychopaths, but there does seem to be room to think that the isolation and introversion that the internet encourages, feeds, in a manner of speaking, the distancing between people. The way the internet seems to nourish the idea that other people don't exist, don't matter. That kind of thing? Well, that could, could, I note, also be a trigger for psychopathic behaviour. But, Rebecca, you really shouldn't worry about that."

Despite Randall's attempts to sideline him in the conversation, Peter kept drawing attention back to himself, much to Becky's relief.

"It seems to me that the internet has the potential for isolated communities to be created, and 'nourished' as you put it, by fake news, Randall. Doesn't that worry you?"

He was struggling for time. On the matter of the internet, Peter had not yet figured out the potential for it to contribute to a new and unique form of psychopathy.

He had read editorials in the news about the potential coarsening of behaviour online. But the idea that the internet might be feeding a bloom in psychopathic disorder, that was off the scale.

Choosing not to notice Peter's intervention, Munroe had been prattling on.

"...And we had a really educated audience, you know. Some of the comments made after the event went into detail on prescribing. One bloke I talked to, can't recall his name, he described various means to assess psychopathy: measures of boldness, disinhibition, and meanness. These seemed like sensible ways to assess what we think of as constituting the character of a psychopath, ways to assess a potential psychopath, according to the Psychopathy Checklist – which he referred to as PC, bit confusing, you know, PC or PC!"

Munroe smiled weakly at Becky, his eye wandering up and down what he could see of her body, in a manner which made her want to hit him.

Seemingly unaware, Randall carried on. "Or the Psychopathic Personality Inventory, or PPI. And then there is..."

Peter leaned back on his stool. *Shit, I'm going to have to go back to school to learn more about this.*

Randall talked on and on. "...But key to me is the clear identification of universal psychopathic tendency. We are all, to one degree or another, all psychopaths."

There, he had said it. The core of Langley's lecture.

Steve leaned in now, as this was the point of the conversation. "You believe that, Randall? You really think that's true?"

The academic raised his voice in reply. "Why? Does it worry you, Stephen? I'm frankly surprised by that, knowing your laid-back attitude to most things. But does the notion of the truth that we are wolf to each other really seem so worrisome? Isn't it our daily experience of life as Langley suggested? That Nietzsche was right? That," he lowered his voice, "there was some essence of truth to the structures and processes of Stalin and Hitler? That the soft, 'nice' liberalism we live with has distorted our vision of what people really are?"

Randall looked down at his glass, raised it in salute to the three friends and sank the remains. "Of course, it is a challenge, but Sartre would probably be pleased with our final and full understanding that, 'hell is other people'. And what on earth shall we all get up to in hell when it becomes our common experience, eh?"

The self-satisfied smirk which accompanied this statement was both stupid and repellent.

"But you don't really believe that." Again, it was Steve who had spoken, leaning across Becky, eyes troubled. Steve had spoken in haste, as worried as Peter now, worried by a world view which had no respect for the vulnerable, the lost, the weak.

Randall looked at Steve with what appeared to be compassion but was actually contempt.

"Of course I do, Stephen. And, if you want to be on the right side of history, I suggest you, and you other two, pull out your collective fingers and choose your side and swiftly does it. To quote another great prophet, 'times they are changing'. Those on the wrong side of history tend to find themselves its victims, its prey, extinct. Is that putting it a bit too strongly? I don't think so."

The three instinctively pulled together, a redoubt of decency in the face of Randall's hateful thesis.

Smiling unpleasantly at them, he shouted over his shoulder, "Pauly, another drink for me and my mates. They really do look like they need one. Oh, and Peter," he added with a wink, "Gordon will be back in a few weeks, on the longest night! I planned it but it is also by popular demand. Perhaps you should address your questions and thoughts to him? Open mic? Q and A in the club? I feel sure that Gordon would be delighted to embrace your concerns. You could read him some of your poetry at the same time!"

6

1 December
Twenty-one days before the cynosure –
Zoe

Swimming up to daylight, the taste of stale wine, the effects of bad sleep and the haunting memory of Gordon Langley.

I feel like shit!

Zoe, speaking to Zoe, and the conversation was not progressing smoothly.

A hungover girl in a shared flat in London town. Not unusual. Zoe yawned, scratched her head and farted. Her 'long weekend' in London had turned into a protracted stay with her friend Alice. Well, as she had tried to explain to her worried parents, Alice wasn't really a friend, more an acquaintance of a friend from school. She and her best friend from sixth form college, Maggie, had come down to the smoke together and Zoe had decided to stay, Maggie heading off back to Norwich while Zoe hung around, Alice's invitation, of course.

"But if you stay, lovely Zoe, divine to have you an all, you gotta pay. 'Tis only fair that you help to pay the rent."

"No sooner said, Alice, no sooner said…"

And Zoe talked her way into a little job at a local coffee shop, charming the Australian owner, Jeff, with flirty conversation.

"Do you really sell kangaroo coffee? Is that like the cat coffee? You know the stuff that goes through and comes out the other end and… well, bit gross, sure."

"About kangaroos, what is it that they keep in their pouches? Must be very warm and snuggly in there."

Alice and Zoe shone with the same irreverent light, and Zoe revelled in shaking the stultifying claustrophobia of Norfolk off her Doc Martens, now experiencing the urban spice of London full on.

She did need to clear this with parentals. Zoe was determined on her life course, but she was not cruel. All was sorted out in a couple of short return trips to the isolated rural cottage which had always been her home. She was back to pick up stuff and to stave off the worst fears of her mum and dad. Her father had been unhappy with the turn in events, her mum more phlegmatic.

Sitting at the kitchen table, the Aga heating the room which perpetually smelled of herbs, spices and baking bread, Zoe said, "Eve's off, I'm just doin' my equiv." Even to herself, she thought it sounded a little lame, but it was all she had.

Sitting opposite and nursing a cup of wickedly black espresso, her father remonstrated, "Eve's at university. It's not the same at all." Eve, Zoe's twin sister, the 'clever one', was following in her father's footsteps. More or less.

Standing beside the Aga, stirring an aromatic pot of something, which made Zoe's mouth water, a small wiry woman, Zoe's mother Lou, said, "I think we probably need to cut Zoe some slack, Ed."

And Lou's intervention had been critical. Zoe could always count on her mum to foster her independence.

Struggling to read the recipe over her pince-nez, Lou pushed the long salt-and-pepper hair away from her face and said, "Zoe's not stupid and she is languishing here with us. Anyway, what's your brilliant alternative? Hmm?"

A look from Lou's laughing eyes, and Ed admitted that he was stumped.

Following a little more conversation, Zoe's parents succumbed to her plan. A gap period, Zoe called it: London 4A while. But Lou could not resist a last attempt to steer her daughter in a direction close to her heart. "Zoe, you still have art school options, don't forget that. You have those two outstanding offers from London schools. You could still have fun, a lot of fun if my experience is anything to go by."

Zoe had hugged her mum and nodded to her as she got on the train at Norwich station, but she had not been really interested. She loved her mother, but there was no way that she wanted to be like her.

She had been in London now for some months and already had all the confidence which near perfect ignorance of danger can provide. OSD had been the first dent in her self-possessed assurance.

The memory of the night was still with Zoe, and, like Peter Finch, she had been upset by Langley's talk, but was surprised to find that the rest of the gang had put it behind them. It was almost as if it had not happened. But Zoe could still recall their faces during the talk, the effect of Langley's words.

The memory was hiding in plain sight but, as hours ticked by, Zoe doubted her experience and began to question the veracity of the recollection.

She regretted not leaving earlier.

And then, why the hell did I get so drunk? It was stupid. Forgetting so much, even if it was horrible, makes me feel so vulnerable.

Zoe was also frustrated not to have pressed Alice about the experience in the following days. But it had not felt right. Alice had no comment to make when asked gently and, if pressed, had got angry.

"Look, Zoe, it was just another dull evening with wanker-type academics. Like all the others. We just go there to laugh at them. Remember? It wasn't a big deal."

"But don't you remember how you felt at the time, Alice? I thought it was a bit scary." Choosing her words carefully, she continued. "Lex and Zeff seemed, well, a little crazy. The talk, well, it upset them."

"You're the one who's upset, crazy Zoe. What are you trying to say, that they got brainwashed by the creep who was talking? What are you saying, Zoe, coz it doesn't make any sense to me? Hey, but I was only there, listening to it and talking to our mad, crazy friends. So, what the fuck do I know? I mean, you clearly have a superior understanding to me, to us, me and my friends, I mean."

Feeling even more anxious, gaslit by the insinuation that she was calling other people crazy, Zoe backed off and began to seriously doubt her own account. She did not want this. Zoe's path was to follow the line of least resistance and it had not been her intention to irritate Alice. But Alice was reacting to her in a strange way. She was never like this. She was usually so laid-back. Even this reaction fed Zoe's worry, but the more pressing emotion was a need to re-establish trust and friendship. She backed off totally and did all she could to engage her flatmate with the kind of silly things that make people forget all that really troubles them. Zoe aimed at distraction and hit the bullseye.

Within half a day, Alice was back to her old self, and they were having a laugh at a coffee shop in Notting Hill.

But the memory lingered in Zoe's mind. She had been on the edge of a precipice at OSD; that was how it felt. She and her friends had backed away now, the yawning chasm revealed in Langley's words receded and became dreamlike. Were they right, was it just a boring night with a dull speaker talking about nasty things?

Looking in the mirror in the shared bathroom, looking at her own eyes, remembering what had happened in OSD, Zoe almost shouted, "Bullshit and bollocks! I saw what I saw."

She decided that she wanted nothing more to do with academics, the kinds of mind revealed in the thinkers at OSD; that was not for her. She did not want to venture near that chasm again; she did not want to feel the pull at her; and, if it was a dream, she did not ever want to have that dream again.

Despite her best endeavours, her friendship with Alice, Lex and Zeff had never been fully salvaged from the after-effects of the OSD evening. Indeed, although her friends had seemed to recover, there was a pervading sense of change. As if some cell or crypt in their inner selves had been opened by Langley, and although now pushed closed, it was not properly shut and locked. Something ugly lingered, chattering to itself in the dark, and Zoe felt sure that it could escape when it wanted.

It was hard to put her finger on what had tangibly, visibly changed with her old chums. It was a coarsening in them. It was, she told herself, as if Langley had discharged a slow-release virus into the air in the OSD and gradually it poisoned the people affected.

And I don't know why, but it hasn't affected me!

She was at a loss to explain why, but she did recall the bearded man at the bar in OSD. He had not seemed to be affected either. He had been so calm, so caring. So odd in that hostile place.

It was gentle, sweet Lex who had been the most obviously affected by the evening. Several days later when she had been talking to him in his flat. Lex was staring fixedly at his social feed on his phone; the conversation was stilted by the multitasking but had concerned Zeff, who was not about.

"Oh, Zoe," Lex said, looking up from his screen, "he's just my nigger. My nigger lover!"

He never spoke like this. It was as if he wanted to shock her.

"Me and my black man are going back to OSD for the next gathering, a meeting of all the cunts. Cunty us!"

And then, as he turned back to his phone, he had laughed, but there was nothing funny to laugh about.

He went on, distractedly, "Straight white girly like you. You're probably not with the process."

72

Continuing to stare at his phone he said, mechanically, coldly, "Let's face it, Zoe, you're privileged and not really one of us, but hey! I don't care and you shouldn't either. Just take what you can, girl, take what you can."

This hurt a lot.

At other times Lex seemed to be looking for a fight. He was rude to people on the tube, aggressive with friends. And now always unkind to Zeff. But the bad behaviour would be reciprocated, and then, uncomfortably, turned into a joke, not a funny joke.

Perhaps it was nothing, well nothing major, not anything violent. And Zoe never felt in danger, just no longer loved, or her feelings considered. She was increasingly uncomfortable and unhappy.

They were always looking at their phones and the bad behaviour was there too, amplified on the internet. It was as if her old friends had forgotten that people still had feelings on social media. At times, there was almost a competition to see how mean they could be in social forums, how far they could push an anonymous 'other' before they left the room, went away, spoke of upset.

"Got the bastard!" Lex would shout, and Zeff, now less a lover and more a cowering subject to Lex's dominance, would agree. Alice was always supporting Lex too.

"Fucker. Deserved the exclude."

Zoe hated this, she did not understand it and, on reflection, could not identify a time before the OSD evening when it had been prevalent. It was as if her friends had been reprogrammed and the update to their personalities was becoming gradually more extreme.

She wanted to get away, and that is what Zoe did. It is what she always did. Her habit since childhood. Rather than confront a troublesome issue, she took the path of least resistance and moved on. After all, it was why she had come to London in the first place.

Her last conversation with Alice was chilling.

She had been in the kitchen, ambling around, wiping greasy surfaces, taking inventory for weekend food shopping, and sorting out a strong black coffee, organising her head, strategies for fending off Jeff prior to going to work. She so needed to think clearly, but it seemed to be impossible to do this in the flat.

Alice had entered, coming in softly behind her, so close, almost touching, before Zoe was aware.

"What are you thinking about, crazy Zoe? What is in your fuzzy muzzy head? Tell Alice."

She spoke so softly, and Zoe had turned. She had not heard Alice enter, had not been aware of her, a silhouette of a girl, backlit by the kitchen window.

Alice had come in very late the previous evening, another night at OSD, and Zoe had made a point of having a headache; nothing would get her back in that place.

Alice looked a wreck. Her blonde hair was tied in a knot on top of her head; she was still wearing the short leather dress she used for parties; and her make-up was smeared. Zoe found it hard to define what she found so repellent about her flatmate, but she instinctively took a step backwards.

Alice smiled at her, thin lips, pinched eyes. Not a nice smile. Not an 'Oh, sorry I startled you' smile, more like, 'Oh, that worked well'.

The smile, some would think it playful, continued to spread over Alice's face. She took a step forward, pouted, put her arms around Zoe's waist and said, "Lovely Zoe. What are you thinking? Tell sweet Alice."

Pulling away, desperate to get out of the small kitchen, Zoe said, "Nothing, Alice, just gatherin' for the day. Gettin' my shit together before I have to fend off Jeff's hands. Christ, I have such bruises on my bum." Zoe tried to reciprocate the smile, but, as she did so, she took another step to the side and away. The movement contradicted the smile and Alice seemed to guess the conflict in Zoe's head. Zoe continued to smile and to inch away. The smile her disguise, it hid her need not to tell Alice that she was going to leave. That she no longer felt safe with Alice.

Alice, sensing something, watched Zoe closely; she crouched, predatory. For a moment the tableau held. Then Alice laughed, turned and opened the refrigerator, apparently dismissing the conversation.

Later that day, Zoe left the flat. Alice and she had barely spoken after the morning incident and her friend was not about when Zoe grabbed her things and left.

She was up to date with her rent and still had some money from her job and from her parents; she had some friends, she had a purpose, but more was needed if she were to feel safe again.

Zoe had not entirely forgotten her art school options, nor the contacts she had made. Now truly scared, she reassembled her connections, extended 120% Zoe charm, struck gold in her search for escape and hastily moved into a house share with another acquaintance, Cat: light, frothy, clever, and charming, a student at the art school on the other side of London. Driven by fear of failure and worse, Zoe reapplied for her place, reasoning that they were bound to accept her; they had been impressed by her earlier application.

And Mum will be pleased, point to her. She drew an imaginary number 1 in the air as she sat waiting for her interview.

Her A level grades, whilst not a patch on her sister's, had still been good enough to get in. Better still, following some Zoe charm, the young, flustered admissions lecturer said she could join the foundation year as a late entrant.

"After all, you have the grades and a great porfolio. You're clearly a person with ideas, flare and energy!"

Little did she know.

Zoe was burning every calorie running away from her memories. She didn't want to think about Langley, to acknowledge that he existed, and art school only had to be a distraction. Zoe was running to find the means to rediscover fun and herself again in the hedonism of creativity without fear.

9 December
Thirteen days before cynosure – Zoe

"So, who is Zoe?" Lex asked. He had the darker intentions for the girl but equally was the less sure of her protection.

"Just a spoiled bitch from the stix," Alice said. "She's gone, cleared out. No forwarding but she was always going on about art school. Thinks London's an Aladdin's cave, can't get enough and doesn't have the brains to see harm in anyone."

"What, not even you, sweet Alice," Zeff said, grinning over his coffee cup.

"Sweet me, no she doesn't think any harm could come from sweet me."

"So," said Lex, "who is she? A no one? A person who someone cares for? She's posh, speaks really well, I reckon there might be money back home."

"Which is the reason to consider her as a candidate in the first place," Zeff replied.

"Listen," Alice carried the threat, "she's mine. Mine.

I've worked hard on every curve of her, every inch of her long, auburn hair, her money, her stuff, and I'm not sharing."

"Won't share, is made to share," Lex said tonelessly.

Alice hissed at him.

*

At Cat's flat, another conversation was taking place.

Cat said: "You'll love my gang, Zoe. Art school is just too cool!"

"Hope I don't drag everyone down."

"As if! Come on, I want you to meet some of my mates. It's just hilarious, most of the time."

Zoe had been relieved to find a recognisable, knock-about sense of joy; it was a happiness which Alice and co. did not seem to have access to anymore. Their world had closed out important things which made life worth living, small things like caring for others and joy in company.

Zoe thrived and, within a week of starting, had substantially recovered her poise, sense of fun, her essential Zoe-ness.

With a fresh circle of friends, she had always found it easy to be adopted by new groups, and with a varied and exciting daily agenda of activity, she had soon forgotten her old life. London is large enough for people to move on and for the new and old circles of intimate friends not to know each other.

Art school was great but, at night, in the hours of darkness, Zoe would sometimes dream about the beaches of Norfolk. But these were not sunlit, summer beaches, memories of her childhood with her sister, brother and parents, out for a day at Winterton. In her dreams, the coast was held in a perpetual twilight, the sand dunes and the marram grass black and grey in the monotone. It was very quiet and a cold, sad wind blew off the North Sea and the grass had long roots which went down into the insubstantial dunes, and the roots, wriggled and twisted in the sand, seeking to go deep, go deep and hold and grow and turn into something new, something hostile and dangerous. Dream Zoe looked up from the grass and she could see dark shapes moving on the dunes under the black clouds. At first indistinct, stooping, shifting this way and that, seeking, she knew that they were looking for her. In the dream, Zoe thought that the shapes looked like the outlines of Alice and Zeff and Lex. But, twisting and turning, trying to wake up now, struggling for breath, something in her throat, trying to breathe and, at the same time, realising that they were not as they had been, now as they turned hungrily towards her, their mouths open, their faces resembled the long, white, countenance of Gordon Langley.

8

9 December
Thirteen days before cynosure – Peter

The Thursday evening conversation with Randall had gone on for another worrying half an hour and, when they left, Randall's eyes had followed Becky all the way out. His acolytes tended to be younger. Maybe his tastes were maturing? Becky didn't look back.

On leaving, the three friends found a late-night coffee bar a little way down the Queensway, just off the main drag, and reviewed their progress.

Becky was apologetic.

"I'm sorry for doubting you, Peter. Really, I am. I thought that a chat with that tosser Randall would show you that you were just imagining things."

Staring hard at him now, she added, "I thought we'd be able to defuse the worry, create the space to forget about Langley and his story. I was wrong. I see that now."

Peter held Becky's hand on the tabletop. He wanted

to reassure her, she and Steve. It had been painful, but they had needed to do this.

"S'OK, Beck. It's good to have the confirmation that I'm not going nuts."

"I'm still confused," said Steve. "Randall has always been a creep. I'm still not convinced that there is anything here to worry about other than a small man with still smaller-man small-dick syndrome."

Despite his worries, Peter couldn't help from smiling at the crudity.

He said, "It's not that simple this time, Steve. This isn't like it was at uni. Randall was just a lousy lecturer who had a gift of making himself sound more important than he really was. This time the man has a mission and I think it's making him a little bit mad, crazy mad. This is a new story and, to some extent, a new Randall."

Steve set about rolling a thin cigarette and grunted. Clearly, he was not convinced.

Peter, desperate to have the full support of his friends, said, "Seeing and listening to him, I'm convinced that Langley and Munroe are in league, there's something dark at the core of this. Randall's just proved to us that he's a cheerleader for an unexpectedly successful event, and Langley's message is bonging about unchallenged."

He stroked Becky's hand and, looking at his friends, continued, "I'm afraid, if you both had intended me to 'get a grip', the project failed. I can't shake off the worry that Langley's message is like a warning, like the world's jumped the tracks or that, maybe it hasn't happened yet but, some kind of catastrophe is coming, coming soon."

But both Steve and Becky remained reluctant to follow

Peter all the way with his theory. Becky, glancing at Steve, made one last attempt.

"Really, Pete? I mean, you can't be sure. Think about it, it's a shitty little night club, a den in the rubbish bit of West London. Nothing that happens at the OSD matters. It's just a bunch of middle-aged men with too much ambition and massive chips on their shoulders."

"No insult taken," Steve whispered with a grin.

Becky, mock concern, continued, "You know what I mean." Then turning back to Peter, "Maybe it's not so bad; maybe all this stuff about caring and not caring and psychopaths, maybe it's all a storm in a teacup."

But Peter didn't hear her. His mind was still racing. He had no idea what he could do about it, whatever 'it' was, but doing nothing was not acceptable. Being personally convinced of a threat was enough. And in a few days, Langley would be back, at the Q and A. Maybe if Peter was at OSD for that, then more could be done.

"Becks, Steve, I know how it seems, but I have to treat it seriously. Even if Randall is theatrical, and Langley nothing more than a nasty creep, nevertheless, their stuff is seeping onto the internet and you have to agree, it seems to get under people's skin? A lot of people in OSD seemed to really like it."

Looking into her coffee as if seeking some deep truth lurking there, Becky struggled to understand the sinister reality which was breaking over her friend. Looking up she said, "I still find it hard to see how this can be such a disaster, Pete. Look, I agree. Randall and Langley are horrible. And they have a horrible project, nasty views. They're conceited twats. But how do you know it's anything more than that? Is there anything to get really anxious about? Neither of them are raising the dead!"

Peter shuddered; an image came to his mind unbidden, a gibbet and a swinging corpse.

Innocent words pulling at something deeper down, something dark and troubling. The monster creeping into the world, a horror beyond the known facts but sliding like a ghost under the surface of their experience.

Even as she spoke, Becky, shocked by her own words, tried to figure out what she had said. Where had that idea come from? And she saw the instant impact on both of her friends. Quickly, she continued. "Look, Peter, if this is such a worry, what do you want to do?"

Reaching out, turning Peter's hand onto hers, then grabbing Steve's hand too, bringing them together on the cigarette-burned, round table, "Comrades," she said, "what can we do, to make this right?"

The offer of 'we', the idea that he would not be alone as he continued on the journey, made Peter doubly grateful to his friends.

"You've got nothing to put right, Becks. You're already about as 'right' as you can be. I love you for it. But both of you, thank you for this."

They needed to do something, but it was unclear what. Peter said, "The problem is the world seems to be mad and getting madder. University lecturers don't act like Randall. Literary agents like Langley shouldn't be getting onto stages and saying that we are all on some kind of a psychopath spectrum. And people shouldn't be believing it, liking the message, broadcasting it.

"And I don't want to believe any of it. But, not believing in it doesn't make it go away."

"But you still can't quite believe it can you, my dear old mate?" Steve said quietly.

Peter grimaced; Steve was right. He said, "Well, it is difficult. I mean, maybe I'm just walking a nightmare away from a bad evening. Might that be it?"

But even as he said the reassuring words he had the contradicting feeling, the feeling in the pit of his stomach. His mother would have recognised it, and maybe it was her influence, her bedtime stories from long ago; maybe there was a key there, a key that would need to be turned.

Peter had the ominous thought that something which should be fiction was alive. That something which should be dead was walking the earth. A memory of something shouldered its way up in his consciousness but subsided again before he could identify it. He shook his head, as if to shake away the mists and dreams of his fantasies. But the worry would not go. Further assessment was needed, finding out more about Langley, about where his ideas came from, about what made him tick. Having someone to work with on this would help. Looking up, he said, "If your offer still holds, it would be good if both of you would help, keep me sane, hold me back from being silly."

"What else have I been doing for the last twenty years, man!" said Steve, slapping Peter on the back.

Becky just nodded, her look was honest, direct, and warm. Peter loved her so much when she looked at him like that. Reassured, taking a sip of coffee to give himself time to organise the plan, he went on: "I think I... I mean we, need to start with Langley. It would be good to know what he represents, what makes him tick."

"I always wanted to be a detective," said Becky, raising her coffee cup to Peter.

"And, if I'm to help you, I don't think that I can add much to your web searching around Langley. But I wonder where those videos went, the filming which was going on while Langley was talking. If you are going to find out about Langley, I'll try to find out where the videos are and what the chat is among those viewing it."

"Yes, it would be good to know who finds that sort of stuff interesting. You know the old saying, 'you know a man by the company he keeps.'"

"And as for me," said Steve, "I am at your service, Pete; I find myself an unemployable counsellor, friend of the lowly and oppressed and amateur criminal psychologist of considerable leisure with an itch to be useful."

*

Peter was clear in his mission. He wanted to learn about the history, doings, and associations of Dr Gordon Langley, to find out what he was about. If Becky unearthed stuff in the various chat rooms and meeting spaces of the internet, he would do the groundwork on the profession and personality of the man.

The first bit was easy.

After Becky had gone to catch up with her life, Peter and Steve returned to Peter's home and, armed with a pot of green tea and toast, they sat at the kitchen table, with an open laptop, and surfed.

Peter hit the buttons while Steve made unreadable notes, "For my personal archive," in a yellowing pad of A4.

The search swiftly revealed that Langley was a surprisingly successful man.

"Interesting, Gordon Xavier Langley has got a doctorate in psychology," Steve observed, "and earned from a uni that calls itself 'one of the premier universities not only in the UK but in the world'. Pompous prats!"

"Yes," Peter added, scanning down the page, "he seems to have practised as a registered psychologist. But at some point, he transitioned his career to publishing and," a new screen opened, "enjoyed something of a meteoric rise."

Steve made more notes and said, "How the hell did he make the move from a jobbing psychologist to minor publishing magnate?"

Peter said, "Well, he started as a literary agent, but quickly progressed to be the proprietor of Outré. Why is this so surprising?"

"Not sure," Steve commented, "but, more interesting, why should a man as intelligent, well connected and wealthy as Gordon Langley, hang out with an abject academic mediocrity like Randall Munroe?"

The question became more pointed as they progressed in their search.

Peter hadn't known much about the literary agency profession prior to this investigation, but even a brief review of Langley's work and life provided images of the unsmiling man at parties, and soirees, often accompanied by well-known authors, film directors and actors. Handsome men and beautiful women. He was the unassuming mega-star behind some of the best-known people on the planet!

"How the fuck did we not know who Gordon Langley was?"

"Quite the dude, man about town," Steve observed.

"It's incredible," Peter responded. "He's been behind some of the bestselling authors of the last twenty years; his agency has won heaps of awards; and many of the books he's nurtured have been turned into films, and one has gone on to become a popular TV series."

"Yep," said Steve. And then to the imaginary presence of the literary agent, he muttered, "Langley, you cunt, you're a winner, a member of the upper echelon of the establishment. So what the fuck were you doing in a dive like OSD?"

Peter, picking up the imaginary address to Langley, said, "And you definitely know your fiction. You are a man of stories. How interesting is that?"

But the more pertinent question returned: why the connection with Munroe?

More digging revealed another facet of Langley but cast no light on the link to Munroe. Among the montage of images and plaudits, Peter found a photograph which struck him as being particularly interesting. It was not well taken, and it was not immediately obvious that it was of Langley at all. But when they looked a bit more carefully, there he was. Surrounded by happy, smiling female faces was the dour countenance of Langley, almost appearing to hide as he accepted an award for a charitable donation to a sheltered housing project which was designed to help autistic girls from socially deprived boroughs in London. What was that about?

"Just totally unlikely." Steve gasped.

They had to do a lot more searching and Peter was onto his third cup of (now cold) green tea, when they located the institution which was mentioned for the award, and another piece of the Langley jigsaw fell awkwardly into place. Key to the donation was a charitable trust. Steve read out the title: "The Open Mind: teach, opportunity, mobility. Now that is a neat little acronym: TOM(tom)."

Struggling to read the small print, Peter added, "The trust has as its primary aim: 'The enhancement of the human capacity to think and problem-solve'. How laudable."

Steve, speaking slowly as he read the page, said, "What's he up to?"

They continued to explore.

TOM(tom) had been involved with schools and community centres and had a specific mission to find, "Non-neurologically typical and socially disadvantaged young people and provide them with learning opportunities to gain social mobility".

Steve, scanning down the page, said, "Look at this, Peter, at one of the charities' events, look at the photo. The woman standing beside Langley, who looks as embarrassed as a vicar in a brothel, the CEO of TOM(tom), name of Paula Meads. She said, 'We are here to help, and with Dr Langley's great leadership and generous gifts, the charity can continue to lift young people into useful lives.'"

"He's definitely helping autistic people, that kind of thing," Peter observed incredulously.

But it was more than that. It made them both stop in their searches, their thinking. Langley's name appeared at the bottom of the TOM(tom) page.

But his role was not as a footnote. As Paula Meads had alluded, Langley was the founder and principal benefactor!

Steve said, "This is like a really sick joke! I mean to say, Langley, the advocate of universal psychopathy, he's hardly what might be looked for as a philanthropic man, caring for the weak and neurodiverse!"

Peter nodded in agreement. "Yes, he made cruel jokes about empathy. He certainly didn't come across as being caring or compassionate. His whole agenda sounded diametrically opposed to anything like this. According to Saint Langley, no one cares about anyone. In fact, all that he had said in OSD had been the inverse of the mission of TOM(tom)."

Steve was baffled. "OK, I agree. I'm really confused, Peter. What's going on?"

Then Peter noticed a list, hiding to one side of the TOM(tom) site, a list of beneficiaries, plaudits, thank-yous, that kind of thing. He idled down the list, and then noticed an institution and then a name he recognised. He nudged Steve. "Look at this, mate."

They spent the next half an hour digging past the gift, past the receiver, back to the likely reasons for the largesse. Peter was going to be late for work, but sod the supermarket, he got his reward. His eyebrows were raised as he at last found the information he needed. Pushing back his chair, he whistled; Steve rubbed his eyes in weary but grateful disbelief.

"That helps close a circle."

9

14 December
Eight days before cynosure – Becky

Becky had, between her various responsibilities at a hair salon, pubs and barista at a friend's café on the Moscow Road, found and watched some of the Langley videos.

She located them with surprising ease. Surprising because, well, why would anyone be interested in them?

Shit! Becky was surprised how awful they were.

Various angles, various uploads, shaky footage of the main event.

Langley looks like a corpse! And I can barely hear him.

All the videos were shockingly amateur – no professional editing here.

Under the burning white light of the spot Langley stood, holding the mic. *Like a lover! But his voice, it's so low, it's hard to hear at all but…* as she continued to listen, oddly, as she attended to the voice, so it grew in potency. Becky realised, that the more she listened and attended, the clearer and more powerful the voice became, authoritative, penetrating.

Despite the poor quality, Becky had to admit the film showed Langley as a man with a message. He was much more impressive on video than he had been in the club. Becky had to ask herself several times if this was the same event she had attended.

The video carried on, hypnotic, when, with a jolt like icy water running down her back, Becky woke up; she had been watching far longer than she had intended.

And if Peter and Steve had been surprised by Langley's background and range of activities, Becky was astonished when she looked at the spread of the short talk at OSD.

The videos hadn't gone ballistic but next best thing. They had been seen by tens of thousands of viewers and the followership included some very well-known names, or the use of the names of well-known people in the hashtags. Becky was rubbing her eyes.

It's just not that interesting.

Then, in quiet reflection, *I mean, I'm not affected. Am I immune?* Then, a cold rush of doubt. *But it's got under my skin now, hasn't it?*

The films were a paradox. Dull but enthralling. Not the usual things to go viral on the internet. No dancing dogs, first drum solos from child prodigies, no wardrobe misadventure for a beautiful diva. No, it was just Langley as she remembered him from the evening, looking at the floor and mumbling about not caring.

Becky was still struggling to understand, the videos and her reaction. *Something is weird here. How does this dull shit from a poisonous stick insect get this much attention? Langley must have got people working on this, used his connections to get notice. This would never make it on its own.*

She was right. The chat boxes were filling up with comments from well-known people making excited claims about the potency and power of the videos. And as they came in, they brought all their followers with them. The result was an impressive number of hits although some of the comments suggested that the video did not always reach the target audience:

"Wot is this about? Xtreme unimpressed."

"Bored ffs?"

"Zzzzzzzzzzz."

But there were many more comments of a different type:

"At last. Congrats OSD. Fine platform for non politico correct."

"BRAVE. Needs to be HEARD."

"Born to make history."

"World thanks Lang."

"Truf or wot?"

And many more of a different, more disturbing, type:

"YES. At last."

"This is who we are."

"Don't say 2 much. This is x."

"Banga. We do. U2."

"That's right/that's me/let's go."

And finally, clearly some ill people:

"Let killing begin."

"Time, place?"

"We R United – scary thought."

And, buried in the screed of messages, one word from an anonymous source, one command maybe?

"Wait."

That word. There was so much more but there was something about the word, 'Wait', and the way it appeared on the screen. The way it commanded. The tone of a word, typed with authority, with the expectation of being obeyed. Why did she think that? It was just a word. But it was so much more than just a word. A chill seemed to come into the room. Becky's hair had fallen over her face; she pushed it back, annoyed. Something had happened. A spider of anxiety had run across her mind. Now as she looked at her tablet, as she read, she felt the exercise become real, felt herself lurching down the gradient that Peter had been running on for some time. This was weird and not just because some of the comments on the site were totally disturbing.

A ping from her phone which made her jump. Peter had texted her, "Talk soon".

Becky stretched extravagantly, yawned then rubbed her eyes again.

She needed to walk, stretch her legs, get some air. She had been stooping over her tablet, watching the line of comments flow past. Refocusing on her phone, she replied, "Soon is good".

On a whim, needing a break from the Langley flow, Becky tried to find readable English to explain the intelligence that computers used for algorithms to take videos to receptive minds. She stumbled on a new term, "Large Language Models".

She found the article about artificial intelligence on a newspaper website. At last, understandable English, but worrying.

Becky nodded to the barista, Stan, and he brought

her another gritty Greek coffee; it kept her awake, but the caffeine did nothing for her blood pressure. As she perused the meaning of Reinforcement Learning and Adversarial Networks, she knew she was at last getting something intelligible. RL meant machines learning from feedback. Adversarial Networks were scarier, two neural networks acting as creator and marker, machines learning from machines, *in interaction with what?* Becky wondered. *It's interaction with us, with human beings. Well, us as represented in vast databanks.*

The Large Language Models provided reinforcement and adversarial grist to the machine mill, and computational understanding was accelerating, doubling daily.

In the same article a former president of a large internet company gave warning that AI needed to be treated carefully; specialists in intelligence were giving the early warnings, similar to those that pre-figured the Manhattan Project and Hiroshima.

And here I am, looking at my tablet, learning from web searches about AI. But I haven't a clue what it knows about me!

About to rise, she looked at the bottom of the screen on her tablet and was struck by a blue line and some code that appeared there. She had noted it absently before, it was where the various pages' addresses were set out, she assumed it was like a small window showing those interested exactly where the web browser had gone. But she was sure she noted some odd words. The beginning of the line had said 'copy', she was sure of it. Other text moved across, momentarily, furtive, and was gone.

Was that normal?

Who studies the small print on the web browser? It was just the idea that something was copied on her page. Was the content copied? Why would that be? Who would want to copy what she had? Did she see the words correctly? Maybe it was not 'copy'; maybe it was c++, that was a code or something? But she knew she had seen the word correctly, 'copy'. The thought came to her, for some reason the website she had been looking at had responded to her by copying something. And that was not something that she had wanted or instructed.

Almost as an instinct to a predator, Becky turned the tablet off, turned it over and put it face down. She was getting freaked out and she needed to be calm. The suggestion that she was being monitored even as she looked in on the conversations of the Langleyites was preposterous, wasn't it?

10

15 December
Seven days before cynosure – Becky

The bored owner of the coffee shop grinned at Becky; he appreciated it when staff turned customer and brought in more trade. He shuffled and coughed as he brought over the tray with three thick clay cups containing the black brew.

Dull days of work and life had passed but the sleuths were back in Becky's shady coffee shop. Somehow it felt essential to find a neutral venue, not Pete or Becky's home nor one of the busy vendors on the Queensway. The subject demanded quiet for the intrigue. The café was perfect for their purposes, as Steve observed, "It's one of those places where you feel you ought to have an invitation from the local criminal underworld to enter."

Peter and Steve were full of their discovery; Peter's beard looked bushier than ever and there was a confidence in his step as he theatrically held the café door for Steve, who flounced in with a "thank you, my good man!". Peter hung his shoulder bag on a seat back and smiled encouragingly at his friends.

Becky's body language did not mirror the relaxed success radiating from the two men. She was still trying to organise her thoughts for the conversation. Unusually, Peter did not notice her distraction, wound up as he was in his own discovery. He sat down, looked at Steve, who nodded to him, yes, you tell the story, and immediately began to offload.

"Langley is famous, Becky. He's in the media and publishing world and all over the place. Famous and rich but, like I said before, it's not so much him, as the company he keeps. That's the really interesting bit."

Despite her state of mind, Becky was intrigued at the animation of the two men. She looked up as, quickly, his voice skating over facts and ideas like ice, Steve told her about the TOM(tom) site and their discoveries.

"And one of the main beneficiaries of the lofty fuckin' Langley via the medium of his charitable institution – none other than the worthy," a dramatic pause, "Dr Randall Munroe."

This was part of his big reveal. But Becky only nodded and said, "Well, I suppose that explains why Munroe gave him a platform, and the comments from people online…"

Steve looked disappointed by the response to the exposé, but Peter didn't seem to hear Becky; he nodded happily and took up the story, speaking fast.

"It's hard to see the reason for the connection, but I, we, have a theory. Munroe is pumped up with his own self-importance and he has a few groupies, mainly undergraduates who have yet to learn better. He has a certain power and charisma at university, but from Steve and my experience we don't think he is as important as the access he provides to the OSD."

Becky was rethinking her own discoveries and was inattentive, but Peter, still oblivious, continued.

"Munroe can provide Langley with a podium, an outlet."

Steve, trying to capture more excitement, interjected, "Now, that's not unique, Becky. Langley no doubt has access to all kinds of wackin' great media venues. But what Munroe can provide is a prepared and sympathetic audience in a small and select venue."

Peter rolled on, unstoppable, "And this is a place where Langley can come and speak to a community which does not know him but is guaranteed to listen with respect, and given the size of OSD, he can speak with intimacy, the kind of closeness you only find in small clubs."

Becky, thinking about the videos, murmured, "Of course. Langley didn't want a megaphone; he wanted a small theatre, perfect for storytelling, for getting the story across."

Steve, noting Becky's dreaminess, said, "That's right, Becks. We think this was important to Langley. The videos taken of him show him speaking quietly, not projecting his voice. More like he is in conversation one to one, more a therapist talking to his patient than an orator giving a performance."

Peter again. "It's as if he were standing next to you, the listener, in the same room. Bit creepy really." He paused. The two men were catching up with their story and beginning to think about the implications of what they had learned. Peter concluded. "For some reason Langley wanted to speak, be filmed and be heard in this quiet, familiar way. This is what he wanted, and this is what Munroe could provide."

Becky, still lost in her thoughts, took a mouthful of the bitter coffee, winced as it went down and suggested absently, "So, Munroe is a kind of useful idiot?"

Steve and Peter smiled at each other; they chimed together, "Precisely!"

Then Peter said, "Langley isn't hiding. He's happy to use his real name but very few in the audience would know of him. He has a message which is probably going to go down well with the intellectual types, but he has to win his audience over, both the audience in the club and the audience watching the videos."

Again, Steve took up the story, "You know, the more I think about it, the more I am convinced that Langley's real target was the audience he had drawn to his performance on the internet, watching the video, attracted to it by prompts and leads from a social media algorithm which the techies in his business can provide."

"Yes, I agree, Steve," said Peter. "He wants to speak candidly, out of context and direct. He wants to sound authentic, different, unique. Munroe's monthly existentialist gathering at OSD was the perfect setting."

Becky had not been paying attention as intently as Peter and Steve expected. She was not able to shake off a sense that all of their online investigations had been in some way noticed, that they might be under scrutiny.

In the silence that followed, as the two men sat proudly waiting to hear her praise for their cleverness and her comments on their assessment, now at last both saw her, and doubt came into their eyes. Late in the day, Peter realised Becky was carrying a burden. Attentive at last, he asked her to tell them what was worrying her.

And this was what Becky needed, not the excited puppies. Despite her intention to be calm, she blurted out, "I've got stuff to tell you, boys. I'm not sure how it fits with what you already have but I'm not so worried about that right now. I just need you to know what I've found. Trouble is..."

And here she paused and Peter, switched on to her panic now, knew that she was deeply troubled, maybe in trouble. His face creased in concern as he leaned forward to touch her arm. Becky did not want that; she brushed him away, anxious, and continued.

"I'm finding it hard to find the right set of words which can really begin to describe what I've learned. It's silly I know but, it was last night. Nothing actually happened." As if to herself, she repeated, "Nothing," then continued, "but I'm really scared, guys."

She looked at Peter intently, zoning in on him as the centre of this storm. There was no smile. "I am really struggling. I'm a bit lost…"

Misunderstanding her, Peter, trying to comfort, said, "So am I, Becks," looking at Steve, nodding for him for support, "we all are. It seems like a lot of trouble for next to nothing."

"No, it's not that. It's that fucking video of Langley, no, not that either." To herself, "What is it about? Come on, girl!"

Steve leaned back, threw a sideways glance at Peter, encouraging him to be careful.

Becky, now in exasperation said, "It's the internet, what it is. What it does. How it measures you and looks at you." More slowly, "Looks at me." Then, refocusing her eyes on Peter, "And it's all the talk around the broadcast, the video that went out. It's sort of gone semi-viral, if that makes any kind of sense at all. I mean, this is just not right. It's a crap video about a boring bloke who looks like a human praying mantis, dreaming up a psychopathic world. A nightmare but, he's not charismatic, it's not fun, or sexy or laugh out loud. No vampires in tight leather, nothing to see really. But, Peter, tens of thousands of people are downloading the video and watching it, and watching it, and watching it. It doesn't make any sense that a thing as nasty and uninteresting should be so popular."

She didn't say any more about her deeper concern, the sense that she, they maybe, were being watched, that her investigation had drawn some kind of attentive thing to her. It worried her too much to say more about for now.

And Peter, Steve forgotten for the while, was staring, thinking hard about Becky, noticing the way she looked for the first time, the poorly applied make-up, the evidence of fluster. He knew that there were things that she had not told them.

All the self-assurance, which he and Steve had walked in with, dissipated like mist. He could not help himself; his hand was on hers as it rested on the table, and she did not resist now. The coffee shop seemed to be getting darker, the silence from the street more acute. They had insulated themselves from the world in their mutual confidences.

Peter said, "But it worked, didn't it?"

He looked very calm now. The urgency and excitement of the discoveries had been put to one side. This, what Becky had, not the stuff he and Steve had found, this was the thing that made sense of the whole. Becky looked up, she had been staring into the non-space between the coffee table edge and the floor, suddenly Peter's face was of interest again.

She said, "Langley has a success on his hands. He has managed to do what a million/billion bloggers try but fail to do every day. He has talked his mind about a fringe interest, and he did it at an out-of-the-way establishment that no one will have heard of, to a tiny crowd of people. And the film of him and his words is now, for a reason which I am beginning to guess, bonging around the echo chambers of the internet like a virus, like a sickness. He has been seen and heard by tens of thousands and, for all I know, the growth may be limitless!"

Steve, sidelined, forgotten for the while, muttered, "Banga!"

Peter looked very thoughtful. He grimaced at the bitterness of the coffee. A call had been broadcast. And the many had heard. He looked at Becky in full appreciation at last for what she had found and said, "And I bet you, his next talk will be a step up again. But what on earth will he follow this with?"

"Randall was keen for you to be there, Pete."

"Yes, and I don't like that either."

11

16 December
Six days before cynosure – Peter

Time passed in a waiting dread. Without understanding what was coming closer, drawn by the softly ticking clock, they were back at Peter's place. Becky, still creeped out by her experiences on the internet, didn't want to be alone another night. The evening, a meal and then, following quiet conversation and goodnights made to Steve, Peter and Becky went to Peter's bedroom, to his bed. They needed each other, the gentle, giving, the reassurance of the other's warm body, glad that this flesh was real, their bodies folding down onto the bed, undressing, kissing, caressing. But there was nothing else to do, could be done. They swiftly surrendered to their exhaustion.

Later, with Becky still asleep, Peter slipped out of bed, went to the kitchen, and opened his laptop.

He wasn't sure what he was looking for, but he knew he had to find it. *And that sounds crazy even to me!*

He could feel, invisible to the world of supermarkets and academics, intellectuals and grocers, the movement of the world narrative, the song of the world his mother had taught him long ago. He knew, deep down, that he was in or approaching the crucible of a new story which was as intangible as a forgotten sigh. He realised that a point was coming, and he needed some further guide, or help. He wasn't ready. *I don't have a clue what I am up against or why I am up against anything. I seem to have selected myself as a hero in a story. How did this happen?*

Since the conversation with Becks and Steve, he had been struggling in the dark with an unseen but terrible enemy; he sensed that he and Becky had hold of two parts of the same beast. But he could not see how they came together. How they made a whole, and what that totality might be. In the café, Becky had said, "The OSD stuff, it's all about getting bright young things to believe in utterly selfish, narcissistic crap. Loads of self-love and fuck-you. But the stuff you and Steve have found, the stuff around the charity and the autistic kids, that doesn't fit."

And she had been right.

Something else was going on and Langley was in some subtle way leading both sides towards a common and as yet unknown end.

Yawning hugely, Peter searched for TOM(tom) and scrolled down the page of offerings. He was working on instincts and on some deeper sense which knew the dark and how to navigate in it. He had no idea how he did this, but he did know that he had to trust it; he had no option.

This was not the time for rational problem-solving and methodical analysis. This had to be an associational hunt for ghost, ghouls and monsters, for that which was hiding from a sane mind. So, Peter turned off his analytical brain and let the hunter follow the trail. Inner instinct knew the way, led by the tracks left by his enemy.

Ten minutes, twenty, an hour. More. The night was slipping away to morning when his finger stopped moving on the trackpad and he let out a gasp. Had he been holding his breath all evening?

Here it was. He had found the end of the trail, the true purpose of TOM(tom).

What attracted his senses was a small storm of pieces about the way in which the 'hegemonic and uncaring scientific establishment' was treating 'non-neurotypicals as lab rats'. The furore had been short-lived and very specific to three or four people. The story had been snuffed out by events and other stuff, but Peter knew that he had stumbled upon what he was looking for. He sensed the deep behind the shallow. He was in the surf of a gigantic ocean, and it frightened him. He did not really want to know what he would learn, but his fingers acted independent of his mind. He searched for the cause of the mini-rumpus and eventually found it. The squall came back to a short editorial in a local newspaper.

The article was six months old and had been printed in a local rag, far from the prying eyes of the national news media. Even so, it was surprising that the story hadn't made it to the national stage. Autism was a live issue with a huge number of pressure groups and societies, stacked with anxious parents, looking and praying for any news of a cure. This was of interest to a vast community. But here the story rested, quietly forgotten, well, by everyone other than two very distressed parents and Peter Finch. A small banner headline read:

We failed but we were right to try.

Peter looked at the short article that followed. It was set next to a photograph of an ice-white-haired man with a stubborn chin, presumably the original source for the headline.

Professor Mike Riordan MBE (pictured), the director of the science park in Norwich, speaking from his university office in Cambridge, expressed his deepest commiserations today to the parents of Jane Donovan (18) whose untimely death followed what Professor Riordan called, "A heroic attempt to help science make a major inroad into the causes of autism."

In ground-breaking research, funded by an independent charity, Miss Donovan had consented to undergo innovative neural reconstruction surgery – the result of years of research – with the promise of a cure for autism as the prize. Unfortunately, a last-minute complication resulted in her untimely and tragic death.

Professor Riordan informed us, "I am so very sorry and would like to send my deepest condolences to Jane's parents and family; we are all very upset. Some of the best surgery and biological science I have ever seen came together and this brave girl committed herself to the potential for a radical cure which could improve the lives of countless millions all over the world. Really, Jane was a wonderfully brave girl. She was an example to us all and a trailblazer. She will not have died in vain. I can assure everyone, we have learned so much and Jane will be our beacon, our star for the future to guide us on our way."

The professor went on to say that the other ten children and young people involved in the research project were in no danger and continued to live normal lives at undisclosed addresses, close to the science park (location withheld for the privacy of the children).

Paula Meads, the CEO of the funding charity TOM(tom), commenting on the tragedy at the institute, said, "This was a heartbreaking incident. An unaccountable outcome from, what was considered to be, a relatively low-risk procedure. We had no idea that co-morbidities would provide this unhappy consequence. I can assure everyone that, whilst we mourn the sad loss of Jane, TOM(tom) will not cease to invest in this promising and vital area of science."

This paper understands that Miss Donovan's parents do not wish to make a statement at this time.

Peter was pulling hard on his beard as he read and thought. He was tired but the tug of his hair hurt, forcing him to focus. He wanted to think clearly. This could just be an innocent tragedy, or it could be the outcome of a failed attempt to mess with the minds of an innocent autistic person. And they had more test cases, guinea pigs available, no doubt funded by the research alluded to on the TOM(tom) website.

Peter thought he could see how the two parts of the beast came together and how Langley was key to both. Feverishly he considered various suppositions.

And none of this explains how the hell such a significant clinical tragedy, with implications for so many potential patients, hadn't made it beyond a page seven story in a provincial newspaper! How was this story so easily lost? Or, was it concealed?

As he moved to turn off his device his eye flicked

down the screen to the next article; it was not related but somehow Peter found it of interest.

More migrant labourers go missing in the Fens – gang masters baffled.

He did not know why he found this interesting. But, the disappearance of migrant labourers, many of them presumed to be unregistered, illegal aliens stuck in his mind as a 'fact'. For some reason the tracker which had been leading him found it important, another trail leading off into the forest of unknowns.

12

21 December
The day before cynosure – Riordan

Riordan enjoyed the hour-long drive from Cambridge to the north of Norwich and the science park. The big car purred along, responsive to his command, and the winter countryside, white flecks of snow on the grey background, under the tremendous East Anglian sky, matched his mood. He powered the vehicle forward, a new toy, a mark of his movement up in the world, disregarding the speed limit, the vehicle cruising at 85 miles per hour, a constant dark presence in the overtaking lane, brooding on the shoulders of lesser vehicles. He would not be late.

As he drove, he considered the phases of the various projects he controlled and the trailing edges. Langley had been very useful. Certainly TOM(tom) was a stroke of genius. He reluctantly agreed to that. A brilliant gateway to those least able to resist. What better way to gain access to participants than via the simulation of a profound gift?

He wished he'd thought of it himself.

But that seed had been sown and the institute was

full to busting with the results. No rush now to find the germination. That was a different process.

Now Langley had upped the throughflow by providing the test bed for the wider message to the neurotypical via the meme contained in the videos from OSD. And that seemed to be going rather well too. Langley had found a perfect medium for the Epilogue Event via the videocast. But the man was a dupe and a fool, blinded by his arrogance, his sense of superiority. He thought he had command. How wrong can an intelligent man be?

But the question, 'what to do with Dr Gordon Langley?' was massing on the horizon. He was ambitious and was getting a bit too close to the project's true meaning. Riordan would need to terminate the contract. In fact, he had instruction from higher authorities to do just this, after the cynosure.

A short walk from his reserved parking space just outside the institute took him to the glass and steel meeting room with its vast windows providing a panoramic overview of the countryside.

His stride, his determined passage, was pure alpha male performative art. His silver mane, the camel hair coat, the minimal briefcase, the polished brown Italian shoes. Riordan entered the meeting room, heels clicking at pace. The room was already full, containing a host of anxious minions. He took his place at the summit of the vast white conference table, the high vantage point of the room. The meeting could now begin.

Ten minutes later he was rounding off his initial points, bored by his own words.

"...And so, I think we, rather I mean, *I* can say the project is proceeding well. Moving into the ascendency stage and no sign of recognition of the saliency of the algorithm in our various target populations. Well, none that has been reported to me anyway."

A glare around the room, waiting to see if anyone had not been keeping him, the boss, in the picture. No eye contact was made. All studied the space in front of them as the laser look traversed the room. He had them where he wanted them.

"I assume therefore, I can sign off on Phase 2b and note that Phase 2c looks to be progressing on track."

A murmur of admiration and congratulation; they knew that was what he demanded. This was not his usual team, no, they were not around. They were back in Cambridge and there they would stay.

The professor was in what he referred to as 'transition'. He was making his way from his prestigious fellowship university post in Cambridge to a 'new and exciting' opportunity as Director of the science park. He was 50/50 between the two jobs for now but would become full-time as Director within the month. Some of his old colleagues, Cambridge elitists in his view, noted this as a form of backwards, downwards step. Not Riordan. It was not just the salary which had made his eyes water; the mission had made him salivate.

Turning to one of the senior 'lackies', he did not bother to remember names, he ordered: "You, Jenny, give me a brief summary of progress with the Foundry today."

Dr Penny Algreave sighed inwardly and provided the required metrics of progress.

Following the presentation of data, Riordan told off those who he deemed needed a 'kick up the arse', with the ritual public humiliation which he specialised in, and closed the meeting.

These weren't the real people anyway. These were just staff, people who thought they had a handle on the development of the artificial intelligence. All they understood was the language model, the deep learning and the neural network. They understood data mining in particular.

But what did a fucking miner ever understand about the lithosphere, eh? Riordan asked himself.

They were just registers of data so far as he was concerned. The real project with the TOM(tom) subjects lay elsewhere, and he was anxious to see for himself how that was progressing.

Brushing off those who were brave enough to try to detain or accompany him and humming in a tuneless way, the director made his way through the corridors of 'his institute'. White wall, steel and glass, blue carpets. The place mixed and matched Mediterranean minimalist and relaxed Bauhaus, to provide a surprisingly sterile backdrop to the hothouse, dog-eat-dog atmosphere which Riordan nurtured.

One of the new intakes of American scientists had commented flatteringly on the interior design. Riordan had put him straight: "But don't be fooled. There is a rabid canine here and he will eat you alive if you slip up. I have my eyes on you, boy!"

The institute was part of the new build in the science park near the airport. The main building was a tower of white blocks, large windows, atriums, and spaciousness. He loved it. But he loved what lay beneath it even more than the aspirational tower.

The sense of openness was disturbed by the numerous security doors. His pass took him to exclusive levels, way beyond the pay grades of most of his minions. He went down, into the labyrinth below the basement floors.

Down here, the corridors were still brightly lit but far less frequently visited.

Riordan swung through a particularly large security door, nodded to the massive man who stood nearby and barked, "And do we have any progress with the zeros?"

He was not talking to the goon. His question was addressed to a thin, young, bespectacled man in a white coat who appeared to be waiting for him. The man was perspiring, flustered, maybe a little scared. His accent identified him as East Coast American.

"Good morning, Director. It's hard to say, sir."

"Well, how about you try a little bit harder and let me know. Now."

Riordan had swept the man up and was forcing him, by personal gravity, to follow in his wake, footsteps a patter like rain, beside the long stride of the director.

"The candidates online, the TOM(tom) participants, they are progressing. It is pan-cultural positive as you guessed, sir. We are noting valuable developments in the simulant uptake in North America, Europe, and the Far East. Not excessive but stable and progressive uptake."

"Well, that sounds excellent. So why are you looking so worried, Fuller?"

"Fairbright, sir, my name is Fairbright. And I'm not so much worried, sir, as concerned, concerned by the active Phase 3 of the Foundry."

Riordan stopped. Suddenly very interested, towering over Fairbright.

"And what is the XenZero doing?"

Riordan was proud of the name. He thought that he had chosen it himself. Xen, from Xenomorph, the 'Alien' horror franchise, meaning, 'strange form'. Zero. Well, this was one of the suite of patient zeros and it needed differentiation.

Riordan was so totally under control that he mistook his slave-like followership for independent innovation. He even thought that he had invented the title for the project: 'The strange beginning'. He did not understand the true nature of the relationship in which he was imprisoned, that he had been given the title and allowed to consider it as his own invention. Riordan did not know it but he had long ceased to be autonomous in any truly meaningful way.

Fairbright was intimidated by the director. A brilliant student in bioinformatics with a PhD in machine learning, he had considered the Norwich job an interesting curiosity with a flatteringly huge salary. He had understood the non-disclosure agreement and the horrible clauses which came into action if broken. He understood the need for secrecy; this was cutting edge science for goodness' sake. But like a man entering a narrow tunnel, he had proceeded and not realised that he was trapped, not until the point that he understood that he could not turn back. Now, he was terrified most of the time.

"Maybe, you should come down to Foundry and see for yourself, Director?"

Riordan rarely ventured into the sub-basement. Most of his communication with the master and the visceral side of the project was mediated by a virtual reality headset which he kept in his office. Work was underway to make the communication more immediate, more biological, but that was still some way off. Direct inter-mind communication would be ideal, for the master to be in his head all the time, but that, he thought, was still only a plan. For now, Riordan learned most of what was needed from other sources. But sometimes, reality needed to be a bit more than virtual; it needed to be tasted, seen, smelt. Today was one of those days; a visit to the Foundry in the basement was necessary.

Riordan was not totally comfortable as he descended although he concealed this from Fairbright, and from himself.

When he had first ventured down, in a rare need to divert his mind from thinking too much, he had indulged in a spontaneous and unrepeated attempt at conversation. He had said to Fairbright, "For a large, modern building the basement levels are surprisingly narrow and dark. Intimidatingly so. By design, I guess. But why would that be? Why would the architect make this area of the building so oppressive?"

He had not heard Fairbright's reply. He just needed not to think about the forbidding basement. Months before, on his induction visit, he had reflected: *What kind of mind would have requested such a thing as this? To make part of a human habitation so unfriendly, even hostile, to human occupation.*

That was before he understood the inner nature of the institute. It would surprise most people. Indeed, if, for example, Gordon Langley had been there, it would have been something to make him wonder, maybe to question his keenness to become part of the project.

At a certain point in the basement, three – or was it four? – floors down, on this floor was the project known as Foundry, or, as 'the pit' to those with less security clearance, and out of ear shot of the large men in dark suits.

A short walk from the lift area, there was a door, more secure than those previously encountered. In fact, it was a double-security door with armed personnel on either side. Approaching the first steel gate, men and women, looking like a SWAT team, surveyed the approaching pair. Iris scans permitted admittance to the inner door. Here was more security but of a different type: two women, above average height, hair cropped short, wearing mirror glasses. For show? Part of the shtick for security people? Living up to the movie model of the ex-SAS elite guard?

Fairbright knew more than most and even he was not sure about these people. They did not speak and were rarely seen in other parts of the building.

Riordan appeared on the surface to be totally calm. Keen to see 'progress' with XenZero. His sarcastic, "Good morning, ladies!" rang hollow and dangerous in the narrow space.

Neither of the women responded to the director, curtly allowing the men passage and then falling in lockstep behind. Fairbright was uncomfortable around them, the 'Lionesses' as he privately dubbed them.

Following the second iris scan they entered a new corridor, innocuous at first but then, as the visitors advanced, both men became aware that it was fractionally off-centre. The walls did not seem to be quite straight; the floor was faintly uneven; and the ceiling see-sawed in peripheral vision. It felt oddly like being inside an enormous white hosepipe and the unescapable impression came that the corridor itself was moving very slightly all the time.

There was no one in sight. They appeared to be alone in the buried, contorted building.

As they progressed from check point two, the distorted corridor became more oppressive, unsettling. Not by much, just enough of a discordancy to disturb anyone unfamiliar with the Foundry. It began to feel less like a corridor more like a tunnel, strangely organic, it curved, and the bends glistened, and the ceiling again seemed to come a little lower. He could not help himself, even Riordan stooped a little to avoid hitting his head. The tunnel felt in some strange way, alive.

Up a slight incline and around a forty-five-degree bend, probably forty-three point five, nothing was quite 'right', a line of glass-fronted rooms were unevenly spaced on either side of the narrow passage which proceeded on until it was lost by a bend.

Fairbright knew that the glass was centimetre-thick structural. The kind of glass you can walk on, that was used on tourist bridges spanning distant lonely mountains. Very strong. It needed to be. All the rooms were occupied, but they had come to see the last cell on the left.

Here was XenZero. It was Jane Donovan. Clearly not dead, or not in the conventional way, it would seem. Her parents would never know about this development in her stay. She was the recipient of a priceless medical intervention, recruited and brought to the institute by the largesse of TOM(tom). A non-neurologically typical lost soul willing to help in the exploration of research into autism. Neither she nor her parents had realised that the forms she had signed had effectively resulted in her making a living donation of herself to science.

He had advanced slightly incautiously and, instinctively, now reaching his destination, Riordan took a step back, treading on Fairbright.

He knew all the details of the project but had not expected this. He was impressed by the progress. Stunned and, although he would not admit it to anyone, least of all the cowering Fairbright, a little scared. The corridor was so narrow, the glass so close, XenZero so impressive. He had not realised quite how successful the Foundry was becoming.

Truly this was a place where new castings were created from the moulding and melding of the pulped remains of the old.

This was good. This was very good and, it came into his head, was it his idea? He had the perfect plan to progress Langley's contract. Following the cynosure, he knew how to take the good doctor to the next level in his personal development.

"Very good, Fuller, now we need to make sure Jane is protected, guarded against any threat. I can see how we can do that." Another thought. "And, we need to test the aggressive capacity of our lab rat, eh?"

13

22 December
Cynosure. Longest night – Peter

A large hand on his chest, a gruff voice, threatening, "Need to show an access pass to enter."

Peter was taken aback. There had never been a bouncer on the door of OSD before.

"I'm a local, a member, I mean, I mean…" What did he mean?

Becky stepped into the void left by Peter's astonishment.

"This is Peter Finch, a fucking friend of Randall's. We've been invited, VIPs, you knob end!"

The big man with shades and closely shaved head took a step back from the irate lady and tapped his earpiece, then muttered something. A pause, then he nodded respectfully at Becky, the kind of courtesy achievable only by a practised thug. He gestured for them to descend.

Oliver's Smoky Den on the longest night of the year, and Langley's much awaited second performance. But the club was transformed. This was not the Smoky Den of Peter's memory.

Despite Randall's best efforts, OSD had retained a certain shabby chic. The billowing clouds of cigarette and reefer smoke were long gone, but OSD was still dark, clandestine. Unexpected things could still happen. Even the people who loved it had to admit that it was a bit of a dive, but the nightspot still managed to attract interesting people, shadows moving purposefully around in the half-light. Every now and then, some half-remembered, fringe band, boasting forgotten celebrity from the noughties, would turn up, the occasional memorable stand-up, irreverent, obscene.

As the three descended, the club was still shadowy but now, the shade seemed more forbidding than exciting, full of ugly, angry noise and unseen threat.

Down in the basement, they huddled together, and Becky had to squint to find enough light to make out the forms moving around her.

Noise, voices, shouting. Figures, unrecognisable and jerking, moving, emerging alarmingly, half-lit faces, seemingly morphing in slo-mo.

"'Scuse me!"

"Drinks comin' through."

"Out the way, mate!"

"Do you mind? Well I fuckin' don't."

Much laughter at the final comment.

"What's happened to the place?" Steve had to shout to be heard.

Becky had no answer. She looked at Peter. To his enquiring look she mouthed, "This," indicating the surging mass, "it's all because of Langley."

Peter nodded. "Never seen the place so full before."

Becky, getting close to Peter, pointing behind him said, "Yeh, and the bars doing great business."

They watched as a crowd moved in front of the blue lights which lit up the glasses and optics.

Noting the three girls behind the bar Becky went on, "Pauly's got some help."

Looking at the mob at the bar, Peter shouted in response, "Still can't match demand for lager and vodka." As an afterthought to himself, *Oliver will be pleased. They must be making more tonight than they usually do in a month!*

They squirmed their way to the rear of the main auditorium, right at the end of the bar with a good view of the podium and the artist or speaker.

It would be a challenge to find a good lean, totally no chance of a seat.

After a certain amount of jostle and a couple of embarrassing spills, Becky steered the two men as close as possible to the favoured place.

As they struggled to make headway through the crowd, Peter had been relieved to see a couple of regulars; they looked as bemused as he felt. He nodded to them in greeting but, seeing their clear puzzlement at the changes in OSD, his own concerns were amplified again. Most of the usual clientele were absent. They had kept away or been unable to gain admittance.

"Who the hell are all these people?" Steve had to shout to make himself heard.

Becky shook her head. This was way out of her experience of OSD.

Trying to see who was about and, looking up, Peter thought he understood. "Look at that," he said. He felt the chill set in as he saw, above the podium, the narrow single spot illuminating the place where Langley would stand, a banner. It had been set up, a flag, hanging proudly over the small stage.

Heraldic, it hung ominously; it set out the basis of Langley's message and the challenge to all the people in the room, the people of the world, a message which would catch fire and capture the most important people on earth.

"I don't care. Do you?"

At the end of the banner was a symbol, a combination of D, C and W, they formed like a curved X, like the wings of an insect, **DC**, 'We Don't Care'.

*

They didn't have long to wait. Becky had barely steered the three to their niche for the evening when Randall emerged from the green room at the rear of the club. But this was not the imperious and conceited Randall who they had talked to the previous week. He was jostled and pushed as he approached the podium. Peter thought he looked unsure of himself, insecure in this, the centre of his empire.

Randall was used to being the most respected man in OSD on 'his' nights, but things weren't normal. He looked to be very warm, or very worried, he was clearly sweating, his red T-shirt drenched, sticking to his flabby frame.

When he made it up into the spotlight, he stared with wild, uncomprehending eyes into the room. Background music continued to play. Hoping more than expecting his presence to impose the usual silence, the usual listening calm, Randall attempted to launch his 'preparatory stuff', to act as if everything were normal, usual, on that far from usual evening. Holding both arms aloft, he yelled, "W-w-one, two, one two." Then, a hesitant tap on the mic. Nothing. No one even turned to look at him.

He clutched at the mic. He was gripping the stand, holding on as if it were the only solid object in a sea of chaos, staring out into the void of the club. He tried again, "Friends. Comrades…"

But the music continued to play; the hubbub in the room did not lessen; Randall hadn't got their attention or, worse, he had it and they were ignoring him. Randall tried a different tack. "Hi. Good evening." Raising his voice, "I'm Doctor Randall Munroe."

Still the noise of people chatting, talking, shouting. No sign that anyone was prepared to listen. Randall waved towards the bar, the back of the room. Now desperate, shouting into the mic, "Pauly, turn the music off." A pause, no reaction, then, "Please!" and, at last, "Thank you."

The music went off and the room did quieten slightly. A small degree of shuffling, some reorientation of faces towards the short, fat man at the front of the room.

"As I said, good evening, Bayswater. I'm Randall."

He may have been expecting the finger clicking of the old OSD. Instead, his entry remark was met with foot stamping and jeering. Shouts of "who the fuck are you?", "where's Langley?", "fuck off!", "we don't care", laughter and hilarious booing.

Peter touched Becky's arm. He could see a tall, thin shape moving in the shadows behind Munroe. He might be a conceited bastard, but Peter still felt sorry for Randall.

He had not realised what he had allowed into his space. It was too late now. He was sunk.

Langley was suddenly standing directly behind Randall, dwarfing him. Munroe was unaware and was absurdly pleased that the audience now seemed to be paying him some attention, coming to order. His ego flared up again, even at this slight change in his fortunes.

"Excellent. Good evening, everyone, welcome to my Philosopher's and Activist's evening at the OSD."

But the crowd did not want to hear from Randall Munroe. Starting at the back of the room and gradually working its way to the front, the crowd were intoning, "Langley, Langley, Langley."

And in among the cries of his name a rhythmic stamping of feet, swelling and joining a chant, something akin to an invocation, a calling, "We don't care, we don't care, we don't care."

Monotonous, infantile. It would have been amusing if the tone hadn't been so angry, so frantic. Langley, huge behind the confused lecturer, facing the audience, never a glance to his victim, placed his hands on Randall's shoulders, paternalistic maybe. Randall jumped; he had not been aware of Langley. He tried to turn, to speak, but the tall, thin man, ghost white with his blue tinted glasses, slowly and powerfully directed Munroe to the side of the podium. There, a large man, one of the bouncer crew, mirror glasses and black T-shirt, took him by the hand as he descended. Munroe was taken away. Purged from the performance.

He was no longer needed for the evening. His part was played, and he might have begun to realise that his future was very unclear.

Then, to the adoring cries of the audience, Langley turned back to the mic, and stood staring, blank faced, no emotion. His face had the complexion and expression of a corpse. But behind the blue tint, his eyes moved, and as they went from left to right, he seemed to take them all in, one by one with his one-hundred-and-eighty-degree gaze. Everyone in the room felt seen. It was a power he valued.

As Langley's contemplative inspection took place, a profound hush fell, and mobile phones were raised as if in salute. The filming of the event had begun.

Steve, Peter and Becky had not been missed in Langley's reconnaissance. They had been touched by the roving gaze and now felt strangely exposed. Peter was terribly conscious of their position at the front of the raised section around the bar. They were at eye level with Langley, separated by maybe twenty rows of standing, jostling people, horribly visible. It took him back to the times when his mother and father had taken him to the pantomime at the theatre in Sheffield.

It was his dad's idea and he had hated it. And the thing he hated most was the terrible moment when the fourth wall was breached, and the lie on the stage took over. The lights in the auditorium came on, and he knew he was seen by the King Rat or BlueBeard, the baddie for the season. And he knew he would get noted, and that the spotlight would fall on him, harsh and glaring, and that eyes would turn on him, hilarious, laughing eyes. Relief for them, horror for him. Then something or someone dressed as a thing might come from the stage, breaking the security of the fourth wall again, come out of the story into the real world, hold him, touch him, pull at him. And his dad couldn't help, and his mother was dead and he was lost in the power of this new theatre made real.

"Christ, what the fuck is going to happen now?" Steve hissed.

Peter was having trouble breathing. How much air was there in OSD with so many people? He couldn't catch his breath. How deep were they in the subterranean club? There were so many side-lit dancing faces and so many phones, people recording, some were even turned towards him. In rising panic, he heard Becky say, "This really is not good."

He turned to look at Becky and he knew that he was catching up with the danger that she was already aware of.

He saw her lips form the words clearly, "We need to go. Now!"

But it was too late. They were trapped with Gordon Langley. The tall man's blue gaze focused on a distant end no one could guess, settling himself to provide his second exposé of the nature of the uncaring world or, as he saw it, his revelation of the Epilogue Event.

*

He raised his hands; the OSD became silent, as if a blade had hissed and cut a cord, instantly the crowd was made still. It was unnatural, ominous. Langley seemed pleased. He said: "My dear friends. I don't give a fuck about any of you."

Relieved laughter and hesitant shouts of, "Langley, Langley", swiftly followed by that uncanny silence again.

Turning, his gaze traversing the room, Langley said in a sing-song voice: "I don't care if you live or die. I don't care if you laugh or cry. I don't care if you stay or go. I don't care if my words don't rhyme. I am no poet."

More screams of joy, of agreement, of affirmation.

A short burst of, "We don't care, we don't care, we don't care." But half-hearted, as if the enthusiasts knew that Langley did not want this now.

Langley stopped it with a gesture and a short, fixed glance at Peter. One or two in the audience turned to see who was being observed. Peter, caught by the viper, could do nothing but return the look. Steve nudged him, hissed, "Pete, it's OK."

But the gaze was brief. Langley seemed to nod, a small gesture, almost beneath the level of notice, but Peter saw and understood.

Becky took Peter's hand, pulled at him. Hoarsely, as if speaking from a dream, he whispered, "I'm alright."

Langley, uncaring, cast his gaze back down to the crowded floor of the club, began to speak, "It is so very nice of Randall to invite me back. Shame he has had to leave… but I do wish to convey my deepest gratitude to the worthy doctor."

A sneering smile, hands raised, body twisting towards the green room behind him, one or two limp claps of the hand. Turning back to the audience, a more sincere smile, no, a more sincere sneer, on his face, "But actually, I don't really care about that. You may know that I don't really care."

One or two yells from the audience, but the response was restrained. This was a knowing group, pre-programmed, on the cusp of neophyteship. They had come, been invited to the club. They did not need to bay on their speaker. Nor did they need to show loyalty to the truth already learned and assented to. They wanted to hear the next instalment.

Noting the quiet, the focus, the atmosphere of expectancy, Langley smiled widely, a smile that now included his teeth, was his teeth.

"Excellent. Come closer," beckoning with a long finger, "come as close as you can, please do come closer."

The audience shuffled forward. Heads leaning back, eyes wide, the event was about to begin, and they knew that they needed to be close to the presence.

Langley said, "Think about great men. Think about de Sade, Nietzsche, Sartre. We are born alone, and we all die, alone. Our short lives are entirely led by our senses."

For forty minutes he continued, a series of dissociated statements, monotone words, to a staccato rhythm. And yet it was enthralling. Peter had to admit that. This was superior theatre. He thought, *It's more than words, it's like story and rhythm and incantation, like the second part of a complicated pattern or part of a key, a heavy, metal key to turn a bloody great lock. To open a door. To release... what?*

Peter felt the pull of the master storyteller. Felt the need to listen, to attend to the subtle patterns, to remember.

Now, Langley's message was all about isolation, the existential conjecture. Eyes closed, mouth close to the mic, he said: "All people live on the breaking wave of the hateful present. We have no idea what will happen next. The only certainty is death."

Peter had never known OSD so silent, apart from a near subliminal, dull, thudding beat from the PA. Even Pauly had stopped pulling lager.

Langley, his voice becoming quieter but in rhythm, lurched onwards. "The brain is the prisoner of the skull, locked in. Our only way of knowing, distorted images and senses. We only know, what is interpreted by our body. There is no God, no loving being. We are alone."

It was as if all of those in the room took an intake of breath in time to the incessant rhythm. They wanted to hear Langley. They wanted to hear it because it validated so many other things which they thought that they wanted. Langley's words rolled towards his theme.

"We are alone, but we know what we feel. Our compassion is a reaction. Caring and compassion, and love and respect, are illusions. We only love and care, for what we want, what we hunger for. Hunger is real; love is illusion."

The tempo of the beat rose slightly and all of those compressed together in the room seemed to stop breathing altogether as Langley progressed to his climax.

"No one cares. We do not care. I don't care, the primal message. Echoes through the ages, we don't care. This at last, this is the truth, follow, obey, eat. This will set you free."

Harsh chords accompanied the straining tempo which supplemented the growing sense of contained frenzy. The room buzzed, excited like a huge, wounded wasp.

Finally, Langley walked into the centre spotlight of his message.

Opening his arms, including the whole room in his embrace, he released the final segment of the Epilogue Event. "Follow, obey, eat. For you are the baptised, and *we. Do. Not. Care!*"

And the spotlight went out.

Silence, then, thudding, classical but discordant, the music, and then, only then, as if released from some dark valley long considered eviscerated of life, a howl, animal, lost. A noise only heard in dark and broken places.

The scream of the frantic, beyond reason, the pack brought together at the prospect of cruelty without limit, the cry of something less than human, released from containment.

A flickering strobe light began darting a blue beam over the assembled, violent mosh. Writhing, knots of people, congested in the OSD, roaring, screaming and shouting; punching, biting, grabbing. Briefly, mouth agape, even gentle Pauly, unrecognisable. The brief visions of bared teeth, white eyes, unrestrained response to a stimulus which was rapidly unmaking them all. The people in the OSD were being reformed into something else, something of Langley's.

The threat produced a response and, involuntarily, Peter could feel, like a rising tide of reassurance, the sanctuary of his mother's stories told to him so long ago. In them, from them, he had a centre and periphery of stability; he was unaffected by Langley's sorcery. He shoved at his friends, urgently, fearing this crowd and their exposure to it, an exposure amplified, they stood like broken promontories in a tumultuous sea.

He shouted, "Quick, get behind the bar." His voice was breaking, strained with concern. Steve, eyes wide, staring, was already moving that way.

Their location had not been chosen by accident; he had needed this before. Then, it had been to escape for a pee when the crowd had been unusually thick, or to smoke or to avoid a boring speaker. They were next to the bar access, where Pauly and the other bar workers would go back and forth to collect the empties. In the flickering blue light, set against the pitch dark, Peter followed Steve; the bar counter was swung open. But Becky was not moving. She seemed captured; Peter could see the whites of her eyes, her teeth. Fearing he had lost her, he shoved her again. "Becky!"

The crowd was moving, seething; some were looking in their direction, eyes and teeth. The bar access was next to the emergency exit; Steve was waiting there, looking back at them, terrified. Peter grabbed Becky by the arm and pulled her through the gap.

Other hands reached for Becky, clutching at her. And now Becky was shouting something, crying, stumbling. Peter felt he was always moving too slowly. They were in danger of drowning in a sea of violence. He needed to do more; he knew he could.

He had not intended it; at first, he struggled against it. A bit like rage, it was a hot inner surge, not sexual, but shocking, unstoppable. Peter Finch had to yield to a power he had not guessed he held.

Unable to contain any longer, he opened himself, helpless as it mounted, toppled, surged from him. It came, rushing out, and instantly the dark moment of panic conjured by Langley and prepared by him for the world, was as frozen as the snapping jaws of a terrifying carnivorous fossil.

Flickering dancing shapes, fighting, sexual, surging. But the straining bodies were fixed, held in a vice, invisible, concrete. Faces grimacing, eyes staring, mouths contorted in the moment of pain, ecstasy and hatred. All were motionless in the power that Peter Finch channelled.

"Fuck me!" Steve stood amazed, eyes wide, mouth open but fully aware. He had not been captured by Peter's spell.

"Go left!" Peter shouted as he pushed hard at Becky, immobile again, keeping her ahead of him and, by feel in the dark, thrust her along and to the left. The dimly lit emergency exit from the OSD was here, a wavering red light marked EXIT. Now Steve smashed against the fire-door bar hard and the three fell out into the club's small roadside basement.

The door slammed shut behind them and the moment ended, like a wall of water, a mountain of stuff, held in verticality, the world crashed back into life, sound and colour. They were suddenly drenched in the noisy dissonance of London.

*

The basement had originally been the servants' entrance to the Edwardian terrace; now it was used as a store for bicycles and bins. They struggled in the dim light provided by the street lights, stumbling towards the stairway up to the road and safety. It was Steve who pulled at his friends. Peter, lost for words, didn't want to think about his stilling of the world; he needed to focus, to get away.

The viral conflagration in the OSD was just a wooden fire door away, scorching the air like heat. He was unnaturally tired.

Screams could be heard from inside.

A dazed voice. "What the…"

It was Becky, but it was Steve who shouted the end of the sentence. "What the fuck… did you just do, Pete?"

Peter ignored the question; he had no answers anyway. Answers were for tomorrow; right now they needed to escape. Becky pulled at him, pulled and said weakly: "Langley was doing something, projecting or something. Was that some kind of code?"

She staggered against a bin, pulled at him to balance herself. Peter responded at last: "He was telling a very old magic story. And…" searching his memory for a forgotten knowledge, "there was sorcery of some kind."

Hands began pounding at the EXIT doorway behind them. They were not safe.

"We've got to keep them in there!"

Hurriedly they stacked bins and bikes against the exit, then began to climb the iron staircase; they had no idea how long their improvised barricade would hold.

Frantically waving for them to follow him, Steve said, "Did you see all the phones? There'll be video all over the internet by now…"

Silence from his friends. Peter, lost in his exhaustion, realised just how disorientated Becky must be.

She had been staring at Langley, entranced by the dry but incessant message. He could see how shaken she was as she looked around her, trying to focus.

More hammering fists on the fire door, shouts, Peter knew that he needed them to keep moving. Steve repeated: "Did you see the filming going on, guys?"

Steve was trying to drag him back to a normal world, where observation and conjecture were just what you did.

"Keep moving!"

Becky, breathless, making her way up the stairs, said, "Yeah, I saw, I dunno, maybe a dozen phones. I suppose I don't know, Steve. Boys, just give me a moment. I'm really not sure where I am."

A bike toppled; the EXIT door was scraping open under the pressure from within. They had no more time. Peter shouted, "Keep moving, Becks. We need to go!"

Steve was first up. Peter, pushing at Becky, staggered onto the London street like a half-drowned man.

Becky still looked dazed.

Ignoring the screaming in the OSD and the panic in himself, the urgent desire to be safe, Peter held her close. He spoke quietly into her thick hair, breathing her in, reassuring in her body, and she held him, wrapped her arms around him. Passers-by would have thought them lovers.

Speaking hoarsely but with growing control, silence fell again, but it wasn't surging now, no turbulence. His power was lapping and easing, the gentle water of a millpond under evening light. Steve, who seemed about to start running, stopped mid-step, looked back, caught in the new spell.

And then, Peter's voice, he told the story. "We were in a dark place, full of emptiness, willing us to join the dark and be one with it. But we didn't. And now we're safe. We left the crypt, and we did so for ourselves. They are in the dark which Langley is opening, but we held back. Becky, Steve, listen, this is important. We are out and we left Langley and the darkness."

But this was all new to him too. Peter was trying hard to remember things, important information, it was dreamlike, vaporising like a cloud. And despite the calm and control in his voice, he was scared and worried for

Becky. Because he knew, she had not been in command; Becky had looked taken. Would she have got out if she hadn't been pushed by Steve? More worrying, she might carry a taint.

But they had to move. He was sure Langley had identified him as an enemy to his project, for surely, he was. And they were missed and pursued by the believers, those now baptised in the code contained in Langley's cynosure.

Nudging her urgently Peter said, "We need to go now. We need to get away from here."

Steve said, "Becks, follow us!"

Becky moved to follow and the three made unsteady progress down the narrow road to the main drag, London, noisy, jostling London sweeping them up at last. With every step they took away from OSD, so they came more back to themselves, established themselves in the world free of the pollution of Langley and his enchantment.

Peter stopped them outside a closed money-changing counter; here they could step slightly out of the way of the bustle of the night city. Peter put his arms around the shoulders of his two friends and, their heads together in the sanctity of their circle, said in a whisper: "Steve was right. Langley was being filmed from many angles and his words were being recorded for broadcast. This was the real point of the evening."

No words from Becky. But she was looking a little better, with more control. They stood, getting their breath. Behind them, on the street, there were people, cars, buses. Life. Safety. Peter was still trying to register, the OSD had become a feral place. Steve was staring at Peter, eyes wide with terror. "It was like he was recruiting and broadcasting, man."

Then suddenly a new insight. Peter nodded and replied, "Yes. He's creating an army. This is like a movement, a radicalisation, and I have no idea how it is working. We need to think, talk. I need time to think. Was that code?"

No answer, the Epilogue Event had disappeared into the soft, malleable material of their brains and there it would stay, as it was intended.

Slowly, still dazed, they made their way back to Peter's house, Steve still repeating, "Like he was broadcasting to the world, man!"

*

Back in the OSD Langley, a promontory in the storm of his own making, registered the noise of the crowd and the thing the bearded man had done, and now his absence. It was impressive in a way but no matter, for now – he would have to use Randall to capture the interesting man.

Langley had already got an inkling of Peter's capacity and he had noted the power he had to cause the hiatus. Peter should be incorporated, included in Langley's hive power.

But now he raised his voice to rise above the mayhem of the club.

"My wonderful, uncaring friends." An ironic smile at his self-contradiction.

The room was quiet again, all noise swiftly abating. Those still able breathed deeply, glistening, listening again. At the front of the crowd, Alice, Lex and Zeff stiffened with the rest.

"Look for me on the internet; you will find this evening, perpetually held in record, an archive, and, in due course, there will be more talks and more information. I thank you for your self-serving attention. You may play…"

Part 2

"For those who had been paying attention, there had been early signs of weird stuff. Since the early 2010s there had been manipulation of elections by shady operators, hate trolls, or avatars operating for them, destroying people online. We knew all about the mass-addiction of populations to social networks and internet 'echo chambers' where like-minded people reinforced and made acceptable the totally unacceptable. Weird stuff. Some world leaders thought that they might be able to take advantage and ride the pony, but no one in a position of power, authority or decision-making gathered up all the threads, saw how they might, with a bit of bad luck or evil planning, be woven together into something new and frightening. No one leaped to the obvious conclusion."

Extract taken from an unpublished essay by
Professor J. Acton. Cambridge, UK.

14

23 December 2010
The day after cynosure – Peter

It was 6pm in Bayswater; the winter evening rain was soaking, polluting. For the minions of the great machine, it was the end of the last working day before the festivities.

With the leaden tiredness which only drudgery or defeat can bestow, Peter Finch, his wet coat clinging to him, descended the iron treads of the spiral staircase. *No security staff on duty tonight*, he reflected. He hoped that this was a good sign.

Counting the rungs kept him from reflecting on his recent memories of the cellar bar. He wasn't sure how safe it would be, but he had little choice. He had received a telephone summons at work and, although unwilling, Peter knew it would have been more dangerous to refuse. OSD's glass door closed behind him like the heavy grate of a cell.

Unsure if the nightmare was contained, he nodded cautiously to the barman behind the tinsel-swathed counter, and asked the question, his passport, "Have you seen Randall Munroe, Pauly? He asked me to meet him here."

Peter was half expecting Pauly to roar, or bite, but the effete young man, wearing a jaunty Santa hat at a coy angle, was his usual self. He took in Peter's appearance and jumped to the right conclusion. "Hey, Pete, bit early for you? But gosh, you lovely man, you look like I feel!" Laughing, he added, "Work not an easy gig today, eh?"

Could it be Pauly didn't remember? His look of sympathy made Peter wince; was his own state of confusion so obvious? Was he, Peter, remembering correctly?

But signs of the previous night were clearly visible, the barman's broken fingernails on the bruised hand curling around the beer tap. Pauly's hair, usually so tidy, plastered down in messy clumps. And Peter could still feel the simmering undertow of the cynosure. Best to keep conversation to a minimum.

If Pauly was aware of Peter's uneasiness, he didn't show it. He said, "Munroe," and gestured to the rear of the cellar, "he's over there, with his usual gang." Seeing Peter's look, he added, "I'll just get you your usual, Pete, with a little chaser, eh?"

Despite his angst, Peter smiled gratefully. He downed the shot and took the lager with him as he cautiously navigated his way through the maze of empty tables to the corner where Munroe held court.

He found him, as Pauly had said, in the dark recesses at the back of the club. There was something spider-like about Munroe, waiting in the gloom. Peter was ungainly as he threaded a path, darker and darker, towards the alcove.

Smiling only with glinting white teeth, Munroe said, "You made it, Finch." Then, mockingly, "I'm impressed. Give the man a round of applause, people."

And they did. The ten or so young potentials, followers, amanuenses for the great man. They had been staring at 'that' video on their phones but now, smiling at Randall, they raised their hands, as if in prayer, and applauded the ludicrous approach of Peter Finch.

Peter stood, looking down at his tormentors, probably as lost as he had ever been in his losing life. Another defeat? How many did that make? But who was counting?

"As you requested," Peter replied, although both knew it had been no request. The call he had received had been an instruction.

Randall flicked his hand, gesturing for his cohort to make room for his ex-student.

Smiling sardonically at Peter, as the smirking young people made room and went back to the close study of their phones, he went straight to the point of the meeting. Lowering his voice, he said, "I suppose I should congratulate you. You have managed to do something you never achieved in class or on Open Mic Nights. You have surprised me. Not your usual crap poetry, no indeed, that was quite a show you put on last night."

In lower tones, conspiratorial, so only Peter could hear, he added: "I had no idea you were a devotee of the occult arts. Quite a conjuration. Yes, indeed." More loudly now, bringing in his followers, "We were all very impressed, weren't we, folks?"

Staring at Peter, he began a slow hand clap and said: "We were all gobsmacked at the prowess of my ex-, low-performing student Peter Finch, supermarket manager and now, apparently, a novice member of the Illuminati!"

Looking around the small group of young acolytes from his current intake of undergrads, Munroe indicated that they should also show their appreciation. The display was cynical, hateful, ominous.

The clapping provided a hypnotic rhythm and maybe he caught the feed from one of the phones, the crackling replay of the cynosure, a jolt of electric surprise, Peter was back in the club on the previous night. Langley intoning his horror story, he, Peter retreating behind the bar, trying to escape the leering, screaming hoard that Langley had inspired, the rising beast. And then it had stopped. Peter had made it stop.

Shaking his head, clearing his mind, back in the present, with an unsteady hand he gripped the cold glass of lager. Munroe was still talking. "But, Peter, speaking man to man, you know, you really do need to work out which side you're on."

Sides? thought Peter. *Is that what this is about?*

He needed more time to think. He said, "I'm not sure I follow you, Randall."

But Randall's smile broadened. The academic enjoyed being the author of perplexity.

He drew himself up and continued, "Whilst I concede that what you achieved was impressive, you have only seen the outlines of the power that Langley and I command. A war is coming, and you really don't want to be on the losing side." Then, confiding, "I think you will agree, Gordon has shown you that he has access to a great, esoteric power! What you saw, and managed to protect yourself from, that was just the beginning of the enchantment."

Peter recoiled on his seat as Randall leaned in, ice cold now, a hiss for Peter's ears alone. "Next time, he'll get you, Finch. He'll pull you in, sorcerer or no."

Randall was so close to his face, he could smell his breath, pungent, unpleasant. But the academic came still closer, a lover's distance. He whispered, "He will envelop you, my boy. You don't get two chances with Gordon Langley, *comprende*?"

Nodding, deeply worried, all Peter could manage was to repeat the word, a word without meaning now. "*Comprende.*"

Pleased, lost in the vapours of his self-importance, Randall sat back.

Pulling repeatedly at his thick, untidy beard, Peter gazed helplessly at his tormentor. Finally, slowly, like thick treacle oozing from a tube, he said, "So, what do you expect me to do? What does my comprehension mean to you, Randall?"

Randall, a smiling manikin, continued to look at Peter unsettlingly, without speaking. Even seated around the cramped bar-room table, Randall was a full six inches shorter than his ex-student. And the sincerity of Peter's words made the big man more impressive, his damp, creased business suit an incongruous contrast to Randall's red T-shirt, soft belly showing, overflowing his overtight jeans. He said, "Oh, I'm not here to give you details, Finch."

Suddenly the clipped words, the use of the surname again, the attempt to reimpose a master-student relationship. "Just to give you the deal, the ultimatum."

Peter was beginning to wonder what Randall was. His old teacher, an agent for darkness? If Randall could be captured then the tentacles of the thing might be everywhere, well, anywhere in the Greater London area. And on the internet. So, right the first time, everywhere.

Randall, job done, downed his drink, wiped his mouth with the back of his hand, and nodded to a girl standing, apparently waiting, behind Peter. He said, "Come on, Polly, let's go and take a look at your critique of Marxist apocalypse, shall we? I suggest we go to your place, sweetie."

Polly, a diminutive eighteen-year-old, tottering in calf-high boots, giggled and, as Randall squeezed past Peter, the little man clearly felt he needed to provide a passing shot, to emphasise his power. At last able to look down at his ex-student he hissed, "Join us, so you and your underwhelming powers may be safe for a while, eh? Langley will accommodate you. But don't think for a moment that he needs you. Failure to understand this, to act now, will be terminal for you. Those who will not be used will be eradicated. Is this clear?"

Peter swallowed hard as he nodded.

When Randall had departed with Polly, the rest of his cabal shambled off to various parts of the bar.

Now, Peter sat alone for a while at the empty table, finishing his drink, trying to work out why his world was going mad.

Ever attentive, Pauly caught his eye. Yes, that would be good, another shot. Yes please. In a world where nothing was clear, he could at least be sure of that.

15

Later that day – Peter

An hour later, after an uncomfortable stand on the tube train, packed with Christmas revellers, back outside his small and gloomy terrace, further west, where the property values fell precipitously, Peter was trying to think, trying to figure out what he was going to do about Randall's threat. It sounded binary: join us, or die. Langley's ideas were like a demented dream, but somehow, he had pulled magic and madness out from the concrete sanity of reality. Although Peter was not entirely unprepared, sorcery was something he had been trying to forget for nearly thirty years, it still frightened him, conjuring suppressed and worrying memories.

As he struggled to find his house key, Peter nodded a greeting to his neighbour Mrs Magant. The old lady lived with umpteen cats in the desolate terrace next to his own. Her osteoporosis meant that she was bent nearly double, her head pulled back at a tortured forty-five degree angle. Peter shuddered. He had noted before, her strange habit of always being around when he was in trouble.

"Bad day I see," observed the octogenarian.

"I've had worse," he said in weakly attempted cheerfulness.

"I doubt it," she answered, as she followed her cats, shooing them back into her home.

Peter let himself into his small front room and, leaving his soaking coat, jacket, and tie draped over a rickety chair, made himself a mug of green tea in the tiny kitchen. Without turning on the light in his living room he sat down heavily by the window which overlooked the drab street. He needed to recall the story of magic his mother had told to him long ago, a story which he had deliberately, carefully, tried to forget.

Randall's warning hung in the shadows, like an unquiet corpse, again the gibbet. He could sense it, a deathly threat. He didn't want it to touch him. He desperately needed strength, power, but, most of all, light.

A flame sparked briefly in the darkness, followed by a red glow. "Evenin', Pete."

Peter jumped upright, upsetting his mug of tea. He had forgotten about Steve.

Switching on a side light he said, "Shit man, you could have let me know you were there."

Steve sat back heavily in the armchair next to the door and, reclining in anticipation, he pushed his long, lank, greying hair back from his forehead. Smiling, he offered Pete the object of his industry, the impressively large joint he had just lit.

"Sorry, mate, but you look terrible, not surprised given who you've been talking to. But now we need to catch up. Have a toke on this and tell uncle Stevey all about it."

Peter said, "Give it here then."

Passing the joint, Steve replied, "So, using my degree in psychology, first steps, let's start at the beginning. As we agreed, you've been down the club, and you've met with and discussed things with Randall?"

"You know I have."

It was wonderful how a single deep inhale could make the world appear a little less drab, less scary.

"And?"

Speaking with difficulty through a heady lungful of smoke, Peter said, "Randall threatened me with worldly destruction if I don't join him and Langley. Simple as that. Join them or, you know the playbook, accept a fate worse than death."

Steve sat back. Of the range of replies, this was at the super-bad margins of his expectations.

Peter didn't seem to notice and took another long drag. He continued, "I'm totally out of my depth, Steve." As he lowered the joint, anxiety reappearing through the cloud of the drug, he said, "I really don't understand all this weirdness." A longer pause, his voice rising slightly as panic broke through the defending wall of skunk, "It's seriously scary, mate. I really wish you and Becks had come with me!"

Steve nodded and asked the obvious question. "So, what are you going to do?"

Peter looked hard at the joint, as if willing it to fix his problems as well as his anxiety. Deciding that more wouldn't help, he leaned forward, passed it back to Steve, and said,

"Haven't a clue." Then, pulling at his beard, he added, "I don't even want to think about magic, about the weird stuff which has been happening." But even as he spoke, he knew Randall's threat had ruled out that option. He went on, "Randall says Langley wants me."

Steve leaned forward, alarmed, and said, "Fuckin' hell, Pete! What does that even mean?"

Peter shivered, just thinking what that little word, 'want' meant. Trying to gain composure, he sat back and sipped from the remainder of his tea. His voice was trembling when he said, "And there's more, Steve. I know that this sounds totally nuts, but so much of this is like a kind of déjà vu. I think I understand more than I am letting myself understand."

Steve raised his eyebrows as he exhaled a cloud of smoke.

"No, that's not right," Peter continued. "What I mean is, I think I know more about magic; I know how to do it, properly. But I also think I've made myself forget. How crazy is that?"

"Like you're your own secret keeper?" Steve suggested, remembering the Harry Potter novels.

But this wasn't fiction, and Peter realised how mad it sounded. Nevertheless, he had started; he had to go on. Steve's worried, questioning look assured him that there was no way back. Nodding, Peter said, "I think I've got to find something I've forgotten. It's a kind of key, a meme, or something which will turn a lock, which will help me to understand what's going on, and then, maybe, I'll have a clue as to what I can do about it. I know it sounds stupid but that's all I've got."

Steve stubbed out the joint, leaned forward. "OK, let's go back a bit. You tell me exactly what happened with Randall tonight."

Annoyed by Steve's brusqueness, Peter reluctantly outlined what Randall had said to him a couple of hours earlier.

Steve sat back; he looked more comfortable with Peter's retelling of the encounter than with his claims for self-induced magical forgetfulness. He nodded his encouragement as Peter stumbled over some details.

When he'd finished his summary, Steve said, "Well, the world's fucked up, Pete. I've always thought that it's run by cabals of evil bastards or lizards, or something like that. This kinda confirms it."

Leaning forward, he continued, "Pete, my dear old mate, you may not be a brave man, but I reckon you might need to be."

Peter gripped the arms of the chair until his knuckles showed white; he didn't want to hear this from Steve. But his friend hadn't finished. "Anyway, figuring out the nature of the sorcery that Randall seems to love so much, and the fascist, psychopathic shit that Langley broadcast, that's got to be the first challenge."

Peter nodded. He pulled at his beard again, painfully now, his mind still chaotic. He thought he knew where he needed to go in his memories, but his thinking was feverish, getting nowhere.

Worrying that Peter's jangling mindset might be contagious, Steve said quickly, "Slow down, man! Breathe. Method and haste don't work well together, Pete."

Peter smiled, his first for a while. It was the kind of thing his father had often said to him, as he corrected his overexcited son at the lathe, wood chip flying in all directions.

Peter wanted the world to be sane again. Not for the first time, he wished he had never met Randall Munroe.

Steve said, "Think, Pete. But slow and steady wins the race. Breathe, and talk to me."

But Peter was still scampering over memories, his eyes moving furtively, as if he were trying to see a rat in a dark room, something unpleasant. What was the key? Words and images swam through his mind and slid away, mocking his attempts to find his way.

*

Seeing his friend's confusion, and using his best cod psychology manner, Steve gently repeated, "Slow and steady. You need to try to remember your way back. Talk to me."

Steve wasn't sure he could do this. He wasn't qualified or anything. He just had a natural touch with talking to people, but it was long since psychology 101 at uni and the tremor in his voice gave away his wafer-thin confidence.

Peter also seemed to doubt the process. He said, "But how can you help, Steve?" Despite himself his words were plaintiff. "I don't really know what I am looking for. This is such a shit hand I've been dealt."

Steve pulled his chair over, sat right in front of Peter now, eye to eye.

"Look, Pete, I can try to help. But…" his voice took on a pleading tone, "…you have to go with me, man. Sometimes I can be quite good at this. Let me help you to go back, down the years, to the memories that you think are important. Tell me your story, Peter, I'll listen and together we can find the missing pieces."

Peter nodded; he was out of options. Remembering his mother's ghostly visitation, what felt like an age ago, reluctantly he said, "I guess we need to get back to my mum, to what she was, what she did. How she did it?"

It was Steve's turn to nod. "I've no idea, mate, but if that sounds good to you, then let's go there. Close your eyes, lean back, get comfortable. Try to control your breathing, yeah, breathing is really important, make it deep and slow…"

Peter tried to relax. He closed his eyes. Steve's approach was amateur and yet, he had a way with him. He did know how to do this, how to help someone to regress, to forget the now and to wander the halls of the past; actually, some of his old lecturers had thought he was quite talented at regressing people.

Gathering himself, trying to sound more confident than he felt, Steve said, "Go back, Peter, back to your dad and your mum, picture them…"

Peter breathed in, his pulse slowing, his eyes closing. He thought, maybe he could do this.

The stabilising thought of his parents, of his father's mantra about 'slow and steady', it brought the contrasting mercurial memory of his mother to mind. He rarely did this, but he couldn't help himself; he could clearly see her beautiful, smiling face. "She used to call me her little one."

"Who, your mum?" Steve asked.

"Yes," he said. "When I was upset, she would say, 'Peter, what is it, my little one?' And she wouldn't have been overwhelmed by a threat from Randall Munroe," he whispered. Steve had to lean in to hear.

But he could see Peter's shoulders slumping as he, at last, began to relax. The memory of his mother gave reassurance, the comfort of her memory more real than the panic. Eyes still closed but nodding he said, "She always wanted me to be brave and she was an adept at stories of enchantment." Then, more focused, remembering more clearly, "I really loved her stories."

Indeed, his mother had encouraged Peter from as early as he could remember, looking for and enjoying the stories she told, in books, but also in the lives of those he met, stories emerging in the small details of each day. Seeking and loving the weaving of the stories entwined in the lives of others had been a passion which she had sought to foster. Her plan had worked, at least in part. And her stories, the incantation of her words, had filled his world as a child.

"I think this is it, Steve; I think we're going in the right direction for the key I'm seeking."

"Go on, this is good work, Peter."

"Well, my mum taught me the power of words, stories, sorcery; she told me about the magicians, those with power over supernatural forces. Even as a kid I knew that they were a global phenomena. But not as fiction. No, she had known them to be very real, not just in stories, and they told stories, and made new living worlds. And magicians could be anyone, anywhere, they didn't worry about gender, language, history, culture, or geography. They came and went as they wished."

Without knowing it, as he forgot his worry, he was settling into his task. The scholar in Peter's make-up, much disparaged by Randall Munroe but salient to the man, at last found some traction against the gradient of panic and, as he forgot about his danger and his fear of the past and engaged with his review, his thinking became more lucid.

"Magic is power from the unknown, from the land beyond what we consider to be 'normal.'" A more ruminative pull on the beard. "I think I can do it now, Steve, I think I can tell you about my magic land."

*

"Very good, Pete." He couldn't resist a bit of flippancy, "*Courage mon brave!*" Stopping himself, after a short cough, he said, "Please begin at the beginning."

A pause and then, in a soft but serious voice, Peter began: "I was born in the dark north of England, at a time and in a place when craft was still thought of as a physical quality, something of hands. And the men and women of craft were silent and strong. Yes, silent and strong, those were the qualities."

He was the only child of a moody but excellent carpenter and a talented language teacher, a Portuguese émigré. He had loved his childhood, but only just survived its early ending.

Peter hovered over the centre of his pain. Remembering his mother.

"She was shy, reserved, slender as a wand, and graceful as a ballerina. I only found out much later, too late, that she had been a refugee from some terrible trauma in her hometown of Faro. I never knew the reasons for her exodus from her home; it was an etched-in secret which she would never discuss."

Steve wondered if he should be taking notes; he certainly should have some tissues to hand and have offered Pete a glass of water. There was more to this psychoanalysis stuff than sitting chatting to a mate in the pub. Peter was still talking.

"I'm not even sure if my father knew why Mum had come, like a leaf blown on tragic winds from the south. He was a very quiet man. A carpenter, and an appreciator of fine work. I reckon Dad had known her for what she was; I think he must have loved her on first sight and never troubled her with any kind of an interrogation. To have her in his life, this most beautiful thing, that was probably enough."

"She sounds like a wonderful person, Pete."

Peter nodded sadly. "I'm guessing Mum found healing and hope in Dad's silence, enough to put her back together again. My dad had a talent for making things whole."

Steve, aware of a subtle change in the room, was silent, but Peter, eyes closed, sat upright, called from an opening door at the back of his mind, a beautifully crafted portal which suddenly opened to a brighter world. Now, as if reciting a poem at Open Mic Night, he said: "Mum was a linguist. She was classical in her mother tongue, but she was fluent in Spanish, French and German, as well as English. It was enough to get her work in the local high school. More importantly, she effortlessly spoke the unique language of my dad's heart."

Magically, his memories of his mother were dazzling, like a lemon orchard lit with southern sun. She appeared backlit with golden light.

Peter's face contorted, as if with effort. "But Mum also carried a memory of broken things, of shattered purity and evil violence. Her body and her mind carried scars. With Dad crafting a safe world for her to inhabit, she had a mission, and she was ferocious in its accomplishment." Eyes snapping open, Peter said, "Steve, I was her mission!"

Steve, shocked at his success in regression, nodded encouragement. "Go on, Pete, this is great!"

Peter, settling back in his chair and closing his eyes again, said, "This may be a false memory but I'm pretty sure it's true. I remember a cool autumn evening, moist and breezy, rain pebbling on the window, but snug in my home, sitting on the stairs and listening to them talk. Mum first: 'I know it is not clear, my reasons, Graham, but Peter must be fluent in many languages. This will open a power of higher eloquence.'

"Dad must have shown that he didn't understand; I can just imagine his questioning smile. Anyway, it must have encouraged Mum to continue. She said: 'I think he will have a power of order, command and control.'

"Then there was a pause, maybe of exasperation, but followed by what sounded like her pleading: 'You must trust me, Graham. Peter has a power in his voice; it will be his defence and his way to achievement. His fluency, it will be like a shield for him, a place for him, putting him beyond the emissaries of hate, that which is coming to hurt him, to stop him.'

"But I was just a little boy, sitting on the stairs, hearing what I shouldn't. I had trouble taking it all in. Was Mum really talking about me? It felt like a dream. Even now, it still feels dreamlike. And I reckon that the feeling was shared, because Dad still didn't fully understand Mum's concern, it was a hard thing to come to terms with, but he trusted her.

"You see, Steve, my dad was a cautious man, but once he had given his trust, it was truly given. Nevertheless, his caution encouraged him to believe in the belt-and-braces approach to life. So, he decided to ensure that the 'boy will have a trade in his hands', just in case I should ever be in need of it. Quietly, in the background, the taciturn man instructed me in the basics of carpentry, even as I drank deeply from the teachings of my mum.

"Dad was always kind and patient, but it was Mum, she was the centre of my universe. She was the one who nursed me when I was unwell, encouraged me when I lost heart. Loved me. Unconditionally."

Steve was becoming a little frustrated. Peter was able to spin a story out of memory and miss the point of the exercise. What had happened? What had led to the search for magic, what had he forgotten? He interjected. "Back to the magic, Pete, how did your mum show you magic?"

Peter, smiling now, responded immediately, "Oh she oozed magic. She was the one, when night fell and sleep was near, who would tell me stories and make my small world rich and vibrant. Stories to fill my mind; even as I cut, planed, glued, and sanded with my dad; even as I did what all children had to do at school. As I learned number, phrase, and history, even so my imagination was full of the glorious stories that Mum told me before the light was turned out in my bedroom each night."

He remembered so well. Snuggling against the pillow, the dim light casting a red glow to her face, emphasising her otherness, her difference from all the other women of his town. The beauty of her jaw, her eyebrow, arched in mischievous enquiry. 'Darling little one, what story shall I make, shall I tell you tonight? Where shall we go together, down the endless brightly lit halls, dark lanes, and long passages of story?'

Eyes still closed, Peter spoke slowly, recalling the enchantment. "I can still remember how I would wriggle with pleasure as she began, the dull world of school, carpentry and limitation slipping away. And she would introduce me to the wonders, the beautiful magic, the hypnotic glory of language, and it was via the medium of the fairy tales of Europe.

"My bedroom, dark and warm, vanished slowly and new worlds opened like the shells of exotic clams in deep, clear water. Her voice seemed to follow me down. 'Think of the world we can enter, Peter. The door we pass through into endless rooms. The world of story is an infinite house of rooms within rooms. There is no end to it, only the end of your ability to imagine, to dream. Are you going to dream well tonight, little Peter?'

"The enquiry always came with a smile of reassurance. I would look at her and say, 'Yes, Mummy.'

"'Good, but be careful, because I will take you to the lairs of hideous mountain monsters, huge desert trolls, evil snow fairies!'

"My eyes would grow wide as the prospect opened, but trusting. I might reach out a hand to touch her arm for reassurance, but I went with her, knowing that she was the goddess who created the monsters and knowing that I was always safe with her. 'I will reveal unlikely tree nymphs and river gods, beautiful princesses and heroic warriors, brave, true and good.'

"My eyes were closed as the words continued to flow, always in the same way. 'Once upon a dream, a river-dream of the past or the future, flowing here and now or far away, my story begins….'"

Steve's voice, back into his mind, recalling him as if from the dream, "Where did the stories take you, Peter, where did you go?"

"I was listening to her, Steve, listening in technicolour, and yet I was awake, and hearing her easily, fluently in any one of four languages. Mum made language the vehicle for story, and so language was the key to the gate of wonder and not the dull repetition of vocabulary, conjugation, and tense. In my dimly lit bedroom, languages lived as story, as princesses escaped, dragons conquered, and knights struggled heroically. Romans and Greeks, Nordic and Saxon, the myths from the depths of time were interspaced with the folklore of the Iberian Peninsula.

"And when Mum told a story, the language carried the magic of the power of the word. And I took the story, the language and the magic as naturally as an otter takes to the river. It was an enchantment; it was like plunging through cold, clear mountain springs. But the stories took me on and on; it felt like I was hovering over huge seascapes and Mum was right, there was no end. The horizon of the ocean went on for ever and ever, until the dark blue of infinite depth met the starry expanse of the sky and all was one."

Peter paused, reflecting, considering the mystery of his own forgotten history. "I was too young to know it at the time, but I suppose I was awakening a power, a command over the essence of the story of life, and it entered via the doorway of the panorama revealed by my mother, and I could never ever forget this influence, once I was exposed to it, no more than the bird can forget how to fly.

"The stories were real, Steve. She made worlds. I went there with her. It was my reality. How could I forget, and yet, I managed it, until? Until now?" Could that really be the case?

Now the grown man remembered how stories lived and thrived in the consciousness of the little boy; they had been as real to him as the world he experienced in his waking, working life. And soon, under Carolina's guidance, he was as ready to tell a story as to listen to a new one.

"Long before I was beaten down into this dreamless life of supermarket management, my magical mother formed me into a storyteller, as well as a pretty good listener. I reckon it's a skill I've never lost. When someone spoke to me, be it one of my parents' grumpy neighbours or another child, snotty and damp in the perpetual rain of the north, I kind of sensed the stories threaded through their lives. I could, if asked or if I thought it might help, speak back to them what they already knew, but in a way which made their lives magical, transformed, expanded to a vibrant colour. My stories could transform the world, make the world different, stop the world!"

The flooding memories were almost too much. Peter gasped. "Steve, I never realised. I was learning. Mum was teaching me. And it was a sorcerer's trade."

Steve had been watching carefully; he had his question prepared. "And there is the point, the bit we want, Peter. Can you tell me how you did magic?"

Peter closed his eyes; tears welled around them as he said: "It was…" and here, here at last, was the point of it all, "it was when she died, when Carolina, when my mum, died."

Steve took a quick intake of breath. "Go on, Pete. Don't stop now."

Peter, gulping air, said, "The month before I began at St. Augustina's High School, Mum died. I was twelve years old. We didn't know. It seemed that Mum had carried a sickness, or some kind of an illness, silently and, really, unkindly. Neither me nor my dad had been aware that anything was wrong until near the end."

The damn was burst; Peter accelerated as he continued: "Then, one day, we were playing in the garden, and she just collapsed, her face, it was terrible. She must have been in agony, and it was sudden, shocking. To see such pain etched on that beautiful face. I'd never seen anything like it before, certainly not in someone I loved. All the strength of the world seeped out from her, my mum, the most powerful, brave person I knew.

"Later, Dad said it was her heart, but I thought it was all my fault. She'd been with me; I hadn't been able to help her, to save her."

Peter stopped as if frozen by a thought. Steve realised that he had stopped breathing and forced himself to take a silent lungful of air. Peter remained stalled, lost. Then, as if he were speaking with an insight from beyond an open grave, "It was more than that. I see that now, Steve. I thought Mum died instead of me. It should have been me. That she, in some way, took the death intended for me."

Now Steve was out of his comfort zone, all he could do was gape at his friend and stutter, "B-but that doesn't make any s-sense at all, Pete. How can it…"

But Peter was still talking, moving on the great wave of the tragedy of his story. "I can still remember the hospital, the grey corridors. The cold and wet, the silent journeys back and forth but not for long. Dad held back the truth from me. I suppose he wanted to believe that everything would be OK. Probably the medical people didn't understand Mum's illness, but telling me that it would all be OK, this was the worst of all things, because I knew that it was a lie."

Peter paused again. The little room and the two men seemed held in a moment of stillness, unnatural. Steve could feel the air as a pressure on his ears.

Peter was still speaking, but slowing, quietly now, his eyes again moist with un-cried tears. "The lie that she would be OK, that she hadn't died for me, instead of me."

Steve sat back, overwhelmed, unable to complete the role he had volunteered for.

Peter continued as if he weren't there. "Dad had always been quiet, but now he was silent most of the time. Our house had always been so colourful, with flowers and conversation, vibrant, joyful with Mum's love. Now it was more silent than any grave. But there was no one else to help. I suppose Dad did what he could to bring me up on his own, but he couldn't take away from me the sense of guilt.

"I blamed myself; I should be dead not her. At least I ought to have been able to save her."

This was important; Steve knew it. He just didn't know what to do with it.

When Carolina died, although he did not know it at the time, Peter ceased being a child. And the ice-cold shock of an adult-sized dose of guilt was compounded by hatred of his self-pity.

Gathering, clearly trying to measure his words with care, Steve said, "I mean, I know children will blame themselves for things that aren't their fault, Pete, but it just doesn't make sense for you to feel guilty about this. I mean, how could her death have been intended for you? Where is the evidence, man? I mean, to suppress guilt like that for all these years!"

Peter nodded and said, "You're right, Steve, it is a little crazy, but Mum had been my world, my worlds. And she was so powerful. Even now, I don't understand how she could just die, and I was there, I saw the moment of the attack."

Steve blinked, caught by the word. But before he could check his understanding, Peter had continued: "Back then, I was too young to cope with what I was feeling. I couldn't grieve, and I couldn't move on. I remember how it felt: it was like I was locked in some kind of a spectral reality, a not-world," he was struggling, but kept going, "where, where the past wouldn't let go but nor would I allow it back to my mind so I could address it, see it for what it was, so I could heal. I suppose I was frightened and just wanted it to go away. So, I didn't really know that I was blocking it. I suppose that forgetting was the best way to survive."

As the two men sat, close together in the little maisonette, Peter was aware of a flood of memories, long forgotten. He could see high school through a grey, silent mist. Gregarious in middle school, at St. Augustina's his silences and sadness rendered him friendless. Children kept away from the sad boy, in their dark school uniforms, their distant, cold faces, they turned away from Peter, fearful that darkness might be catching. A foretaste of a plague.

Previously a large presence in class, the magic storyteller, now his schoolmates deserted him and his teachers shook their heads; they thought that they understood why he had become a perennial underperformer, living in a microclimate of grief. School was background, and when he was there it was as if sound and colour were muted. Peter did school in sepia tint.

Peter said, as if speaking to himself, "At home, Dad would stay in his workshop until late. He tried to make sure that the basics were covered. There was food on the table, a fresh school uniform at the start of the week; the house was reasonably clean. I was looked after; the weekly shopping was done, we would do this together, always in silence, always late in the evening to avoid any chance meeting with our neighbours."

Steve shuddered as Peter's story took on life and drew him in.

Peter said, "And there were no stories. Neither of us had the heart to attempt to recreate that. Everything was muted. When Dad and I were together, quiet rained on the house like a biblical deluge. I was drenched in silent desolation. So, I did the only thing I could do to stop my sadness – I stopped the world."

Steve jolted out of his listening. "How the hell did you do it, Peter?"

*

"It was my first time, my first conjuration. It's the core of what I have tried to forget.

"I stopped the world for the first time then, because it was unbearable. Like in OSD but it was a reaction. Again, I was under attack – what had killed my mum, now came for me."

Steve's eyebrows had nowhere higher to go; they remained lost in his hairline.

Peter remembered it so clearly now. Now he was really opening himself because he had to, because the other option was Randall, Langley and death.

His mother was dead and he, the child, held himself to blame, accountable, for not even noticing her pain. His father was in his workshop; he was home alone in his bedroom, looking out of his window at the shabby grey street.

"I just wanted it all to stop. I couldn't bear it anymore. My dad's sadness, the endless sadness of the world. I just wanted it to stop; I wanted a new story to begin, not this terrible story of guilt and loss. But something happened in some deep part of my brain; I could almost hear a 'click', as if a locked door was opened. A dark door opening onto utter blackness.

"One moment I was looking out of the window, then, as if a film was removed from my eyes, I became terribly aware of my isolation, how very alone I was. No Mum now, no Dad to help me. I felt incredibly vulnerable, giddy. The view from my window was suddenly huge, telescoped upwards; it felt as if I was in a crow's nest and down below me in the street of our little town, everything was moving, a vast dark and restless ocean. It was like I was entering a story. With a jolt, the shadowy, autumnal street flooded up to me, crowding in, homes and shops, cars, pavements, and people – mountainous gloomy shapes, seemingly made of some mobile grey substance, rolling right up, lapping at the window ledge of my bedroom, smothering me. Drowning me.

"That was it, Steve, suddenly I knew that there was a darkness in me, or in the world, or in both. But I had the power to release it, to let it out, and if I did, then a new magical story would break through, a horror story, a story of power and darkness. I was caught by it, by this release of power, but my reaction was instinctive. The power that I had felt from Mum, that I had denied since she died, but that was also within me, it was an act of sorcery; I see that now. Not knowing how, I stopped everything. I stopped the story of the dark which I had released, stopped it from becoming real."

It was like a cold wind blew through the dark little room. Steve shivered and looked over his shoulder, wondering if someone had opened the front door. Confused and worried he asked, "You mean, like last night, you just stopped the world from moving, Peter?"

A long pause. Steve's eyes darted about, searching his friend's face for the answer. Peter simply nodded. Steve said, "How crazy is that? I mean to say, if I hadn't been with you at the OSD I would just say you were mad, going nuts."

Steve sounded rattled, as if this further evidence of weirdness was one step too far. "This is seriously creepy, Pete, and you were only a kid. Christ, man! How long did it last?"

"Not for long, only for a short time, for no time. And, in that pause, that time of no time, I remember blurting out: 'How am I doing this?' I had got up; I was standing, looking out of the window, framed, backlit, obvious to anyone down below, if they had been able to raise their heads and look."

Peter halted and swallowed deeply. Steve was shaking; he went to offer his friend the glass of water but then drank it himself. He muttered, "I need a stronger drink than this!"

But Peter didn't hear him; he needed to continue now, and it was hard, getting harder. He didn't seem aware of the growing panic in his friend. "The power that made the horror story was back, it was there in the OSD, I see that now. The cause of the attack that had led to my response, it was there, Steve. Maybe it's here too? Like an unclean, undead thing, swaying and gibbering; I knew it from the stories Mum told, the stories of monsters. But she was not there to help me; she couldn't protect me."

Again, Steve looked around the dark room.

"And, Steve, it wasn't just 'out there' in the world. No, it was way down in my mind. Something very deep, fathoms down in the darkness of the basement of my consciousness, but it was very aware; it heard me and

I could hear it, just like I heard it again in the OSD, through Langley. I heard it, even if it could not be seen; it flexed and slithered, and spoke quietly, wickedly, to me; it wanted me to join it, the monster, the whisper of a corpse!"

Steve was wide eyed; he clutched the glass as if it were there to protect him; his hairline was drenched with sweat. Peter was struggling with the story, with the memory, unaware of Steve's terror. Steve managed to lean forward, give his shoulder a squeeze, despite his fear, encouraging his friend to go on, to get to the end.

"I remember staggering under the attack, I think I said something like, 'I hate this story', or maybe it was, 'get away from me!'. Then I felt a shudder, like a small earthquake or something, and the two spells – the horror and the stopping spell – they were broken. And the world roared back into traffic-screeching, child-shouting life."

Steve sat back; his breathing was shallow. "I reckon your mum was some kind of a shaman or something. With her stories, she opened up a channel, a doorway." He was scaring himself. "And it got her and, well, you drew whatever it was to you. It was in you too, and it rose up to get you, to get us all!"

Peter shuddered but Steve was really panicking now.

"You're like some kind of a magnet, Pete. And it all happened again, back in the OSD! You drew the power to you, the evil behind that cunt Langley."

Peter nodded and said, "But I withstood the attack. I controlled the attack, shut it down."

Steve took this in but was clearly still very worried. He said, "What scares the shit out of me, man, I mean,

I'm still wondering where the attack came from in the first place and, more pertinently, what had you done?"

Steve's eyes were darting around the dark room again, as if he was expecting some new manifestation. He continued, "How did you manage to push it back? Christ, man, you just seem to open yourself to the attacks. This is super scary, Pete. I'm not sure I can deal with this even if you get really good at stopping the world. We were all attacked."

Peter nodded. "Yes, I see that, and my rejection, my spell, it was more by luck than any kind of mastery."

"Well," Steve responded, "Pete, this is too much for me. You'd better get some mastery and quickly." He was fidgeting; he clearly wanted it all to end. "And I reckon that the OSD display was just the tip of a huge iceberg of esoteric nastiness. What Langley has, it may even be the same kind of magic you experienced as a child, that your mum understood. It seems to be governing and controlling Randall Munroe, and Langley is more than ready to waylay you again. What the fuck are you going to do?"

Peter nodded again. He noted the use of 'you'. Not 'we' now.

Steve was too shaken. This was bad and he was talking himself into a major anxiety attack.

Shaking his head, Peter said, "It's going to be OK, Steve. I know the source now. In the OSD at Langley's second talk, the power, the magic, was out of sight and deep down, subliminal, but all the more real for that. Through Langley, it was playing with me, demonstrating what it could do – make people crazy. Letting me know in advance how it could mess with me if I refused the invitation which Randall would deliver.

"The point is, Steve, now that I've remembered how my magic began, how the story began, I know that the spell of stopping is something I can do. Don't you see, this changes things?"

"I don't know, Pete, but I don't think I'm up for this. Sorry, mate, but you're on your own now. I can't handle this kind of shit."

And with that Steve left Peter and went back to his room. The closing and then locking of his door sounded ominous.

16

2011
Zoe

Zoe was doing what she did well, breaking away, forgetting the past and making a fresh start in a new world.

When she left the flat, she had also cut herself off from the social group around Alice and Zeff and Lex and she was relieved. Each day was a day of forgetful healing. But even if she felt thankful not to have them in her life anymore, as she tried to forget all about the weirdness associated with them, dismiss it as some kind of an illusion, even so, she was no penitent. As she said to herself, *That was then, this is now. The Zoe party must go on!*

Christmas with her new mates had been a blur of forgetful fun. All too soon it was January – grey skies, cold, drizzle – Christmas parties felt like a lifetime, not just a few days, ago. London in 2011. But if the weather was meh, it didn't affect Zoe. She had been in a pre-semester preparatory class on art history in the Fine Arts Building, known to all as FAB. She attended with Cat and a couple of female friends. Following the lecture on Caravaggio, she and her friends headed off, across the university square, making their way to their next class. Conversation was very Zoe.

"So, he was gay but also a murderer and a paedophile and he did tonnes of religious stuff for cardinals and popes and the like. Who'd've thought!"

"They were all like that. Actually, *all* men are like that."

"Such a gross generalisation."

"Nope, those Medici and all that."

"That's just TV."

"So what? TV is truth, lady! Main thing is, they had a lot of fun."

General laughter but then, mid-nonsense, Zoe noticed a familiar face on the other side of the square, moving urgently, apparently heading back, towards FAB.

It was Alice.

Zoe stopped and looked again. Yes, it was her old friend and flatmate but, something was not right. There was something feral, wild and hostile about her, something that Zoe could not initially describe. It was Alice but this was not the fun, carefree Alice she had first met with Maggie. This was a continuation of the Alice in the kitchen, the Alice of teeth and no smile. Someone who looked like they slept in their clothes, the woman who had terrified her. Instinctively Zoe ducked behind the three other girls, allowing them to shield her from Alice's view. Cat noticed and asked, "OK, Zoe?"

"Yes, sure, just thought I had mislaid a file."

Looking up and noting that Alice had now disappeared into FAB, Zoe thought: *What the fuck is Alice doing here?*

On the spur of the moment, she made a decision. Providing her friends with a paper-thin excuse about a question for the lecturer, she headed back to the Fine Arts Building, following Alice.

Zoe was careful; for some reason which she could not articulate to herself, she did not want her ex-flatmate to see her.

London is a big city; most people are anonymous to each other, and friends rarely bump into each other by accident. And Alice had no reason, which Zoe could fathom, to be at the campus. Alice had no interest in the study of art.

Approaching the building, Zoe noticed Alice through the glass doors – she was talking to a member of staff and being directed back to the lecture theatre where Caravaggio had so recently been reduced to a cliché of sex and politics.

Is she looking for me? Tracking me? Zoe wondered.

Why? Why would Alice be seeking Zoe? Of course, it could be innocent. An old friend wanting to find out how a chum is doing in her new world. But Zoe dismissed this out of hand. Alice would not do that. She was looking for Zoe for some other reason. A reason she did not know, and this was not a comforting thought.

It became a game. It was surprisingly easy for Zoe to play; she was good at it.

Alice was tunnel visioned in her search. Zoe kept a good distance behind her but had little trouble avoiding eye contact. As she followed her from building to building, from coffee shop to lecture theatre, she noticed that Alice was holding her phone like a knife, firmly in her left hand.

Odd. It would be so easy for someone to steal it, but Alice didn't seem to care.

And Zoe still had no idea why Alice was at her university. She had paid up her rent; she had taken her stuff when she left; and she had made no mess. Why would Alice want to see her?

Eventually, Alice exhausted her search and, with a determined, robotic turn, set off from the campus. Zoe followed at a discrete distance.

Alice took no bus and she walked past the tube station. She walked on. Again, this was odd. Alice had never been a great walker. She would always take a lift, catch a bus or tube if she could. And the shoes she was wearing, they were more for a night out than a long walk. Her cadence was uncomfortable, painful even. Zoe couldn't stop herself; she continued to follow. They walked for over an hour; Zoe began to guess where she was being taken.

Eventually, they entered a small street in West London, off the Bayswater Road and, as Zoe had thought, as she had feared, Alice descended the stairway off the pavement, down into Oliver's Smoky Den.

Zoe stopped, twenty metres from the staircase, unsure what to do next.

"Hi, Zoe."

"Yeah hi! Long time no see, little Zoey Zo Zo."

The voices, voices she knew, they were behind her. Turning, caught in the act of spying on Alice, Zoe was startled to see Lex and Zeff grinning at her.

*

"I need to know if this is a virus, a bug or whatever?"

Becky was having terrible trouble with her tablet.

"What're the symptoms, lady, I still ain't seen 'em."

She was standing at the glass counter, talking to a bored, gangling youth in a black T-shirt, at the local Mr TechFix store in Notting Hill. She had become anxious about the way in which her tablet was working. Since she had trawled the net for the Langley talk, subtle, and at times more noticeable, changes had been taking place.

Laughing, to suggest that she might be making a fuss about nothing, she replied, "I dunno. The thing just gets slow at times. Sometimes I see text on the browser screen which I don't understand. I get little messages appearing in boxes and then they go away, that kinda thing."

"What sort of messages?" He picked the tablet up, looked at it more intently. This was a bit more interesting. This was not the usual obvious virus scare.

"Dunno. They come and go so quick. They just flick up and down."

Becky had a feeling that the messages were intended to be subliminal, for unconscious registering in the unsuspecting brain. She felt sure that her tablet was infected in some way and was doing something to her, trying to program her, but she did not know what to do about it or even where to start. Peter was hopeless at this, worse than her. He was anxious all the time about passwords, security, and trolls. It said a lot about his overall lack of technology understanding that he had been more than happy for her to look at the Langley video, to trawl that wave. Anyway, he was preoccupied with his continuing survey of Langley's empire.

The youth had lost interest in the project again.

"I'll do a scan for you, give it a health check. Take about an hour. Forty quid. OK?"

"Sure."

And she paid in cash and left the unlocked tablet with him. It was a relief not to have it with her. Since she had begun her online search for Langley, she had morbid worries about the thing. She worried about it looking at her, rather than her controlling it.

But that was not all that Becky was feeling shit about that morning.

It was in her head. The face, the long face of Langley. Since the second gig, the bar, the dark, the words about death and life and not caring. She had not been sleeping well. And, despite her reservations about her technology, she found herself looking at it, looking at the videos of Langley and, *tuning out, turning my brain off*.

And this was alarming. She would find herself sitting on her couch, tablet in hand, screen blank. And she did not know how long she had been like that.

And then there were the dreams.

They had begun with corridors – long, grey corridors – and pursuit. Most people have dreamed a bit like that, being chased and going slower and slower. But these dreams were different. Becky felt like she was being chased by a dark presence which slid and twittered in the dark behind her, and in the dream Becky was looking for a room, her room, a room where she would be safe for ever. She did not want to be in the corridors, she did not want to find the room, but both were preferrable to being caught by the pursuing things.

Another dream followed on from the corridor dream, as she came to call it.

In the second dream she was looking for someone or something. It was dark and she could hear the sea, but she was not sure of the sand under her feet. She needed to find someone, but she could not see. Then, and it was always the same, she would hear Peter and he would be singing, and she would feel better, but the sand slid away, and she fell and fell and woke.

Becky had felt lonely and a bit vulnerable since Langley's second talk at the OSD. Of course, Pete and Steve and she had spoken, talked a lot. But Peter had his day job and, anyway, was totally preoccupied. As for Steve, he was doing a lot of skunk. He seemed hell bent on forgetting about everything they had done. They just didn't have a plan. When she talked to Peter about her worries, he was testy.

"I'm not sure what I can do, Becky. I'm out of my depth. I'm not a magician. Becks, this is so oblique, dark, insubstantial. I'm not even sure that there really is some big, monstrous thing happening. I told Steve, I need time to think, Becks. And work is really busy, and I just don't have time to orientate myself to this."

It was so unlike Pete. He had left her. And in leaving her he left her with all the problems that had come as a consequence of his needing her help. Now she needed help. *And he doesn't seem to care*, she thought.

This was very hard. She always looked out for Pete, and he had been in deep need. But now, as the consequences of horror continued to form and multiply in her life, in her mind, in her dreams, Peter was 'busy' and Steve was stoned.

I'll just have to sort myself out.

The first thing had been the tablet. She was glad it was being looked at. That was one part of her life she could control and didn't need Peter for.

She had been making her way home, her walk took her past the side road where OSD brooded under a terrace of Edwardian shops.

Becky had no wish to get any closer to the club but, glancing up the road, she saw what looked like a struggle going on by the spiral staircase. Becky had been around London long enough to know to keep clear of shouting men near bars but what made her stop and turn on this occasion was the frightened voice of a young woman.

Two young men had a girl. One held her by the arms; the other clutched a handful of her hair. They were dragging her towards the club steps.

Becky used maximum volume as she shouted: "What the fuck are you two twats doing? Leave the girl alone."

Other pedestrians walking nearby, apparently ignoring the young girl and her struggle, now stopped and took notice.

Becky had the odd feeling that she recognised the woman, a young girl, maybe eighteen or so, pretty, with thick, auburn hair. She looked terrified. Another woman, a mousy blonde, was on the stairs laughing. It was the laugh, pitiless and unkind, that crossed a wire in Becky's brain; it made her really angry.

Shouting now, top of her voice, the kind of shout Becky would use if she felt herself in a bit of bother and wanted to wake an entire neighbourhood at two in the morning.

"I said leave that kid alone, you fuckers!"

She was walking briskly towards them, her shoes making a rhythmic tap on the pavement.

Disturbed, the two men looked up, annoyed at the interruption but still mocking. The blonde shouted something rude, and the two young men, unkempt and dirty, snarled at her, not like people, like animals.

Becky did not have time to feel scared. It was broad daylight in West London and these people were trying to mug a young girl. Becky was in her rights and mad. And she had a secret weapon. Even as she advanced on the group, and the young men looked at her, holding the struggling girl, still contemptuous, Becky Mace'd them. The aerosol of Mace, strictly illegal in the UK, was an indispensable aid for women in cities from Becky's point of view. She took some delight in giving each of the men a fairly intense shot in the face; the effect was immediate and gratifying.

The men dropped the girl who fell onto the pavement; they held their hands up to their faces, shouting in pain and shock.

Becky, on them now, kicked one in the balls and shouted: "Be a lesson to you, you bastards! Now fuck off!"

The two began to stagger away. Zoe looked wild with fright. The blonde had disappeared down into the club.

"You alright? Did they hurt you?"

Becky put out her hand and helped the girl to her feet.

"You OK?" Becky repeated, but the girl was backing away with her hand up to her mouth. Zoe shouted something but Becky didn't hear it because everything went dark.

17

Randall

Randall was irritated. He did not like violence, other than the elegantly inoffensive type, to be found in novels of a literary genre. Theory was enough for him. He would have gladly agreed to the hanging of the monarch but would not want to be anywhere near it when it happened. He was a radical intellectual after all.

Now he had been called into action to quieten Peter's friend Rebecca. What made it worse was that he fancied her, had wanted to get into her knickers and now felt he had probably ruined his chances. He was confused and worried, initially at a low level.

Randall was confused by many things nowadays.

There were large parts of his day which he did not remember, and he did not even seem to want to remember. He was content to be blank. And sometimes he would find himself just sitting. At his home or on a tube or, more alarmingly, at a coffee shop with a barista shaking him and telling him to buy something or go.

"You can't just come in here and go to sleep, mate. It's not a hotel."

He would find himself in strange bits of London. Bits he did not recall ever coming to before. Sometimes he was with strangers, and they were all dirty, sweaty. And he had no idea what he had been doing to get so out of breath.

Today, he realised he had just abducted Rebecca in broad daylight on a London street and was dragging her, in full view of some alarmed pedestrians, into the OSD. He was helped by the pasty blonde girl. And he knew he had failed in some way.

The other girl. The lovely, frightened brunette, she had put her head down and run off. Just set off like a hare damn it. Rebecca had messed things up for him, coming up like that. Damn her too, she deserved to be chloroformed.

Then the thought, Langley would not be happy.

Langley would like the fact that they had Rebecca. He had mentioned her. But the prize was supposed to be the brunette, that was who he was waiting for. Randall was very frightened. Not of the consequences of police or any of that sort of thing, that could be made to go away. No, he knew that he did not want to enrage Langley, but he did not have the mental energy to get very upset about that. And this surprised him.

And then Langley turned up and had been very angry. And Randall had just stood and let him hit him in the mouth, again and again. And he fell down, and he could taste blood and he felt sure one of his teeth was loosened. And Langley used his feet too. Kicking slowly, accurately. Methodically. All over, particularly in the head. Randall observed the concussions, the pain, the humiliation in the small part of his mind which was still his. And it had hurt a lot.

And the others, the others in the OSD, had stood and watched, grinning. Enjoying. But he had not shouted or cried out. And this surprised him because he was not a strong man or a brave person. He hated pain. But this was not a pain he could avoid. And, when Langley had finished kicking and punching, the tall man became very calm. Breathing hard, he told Randall in a very matter-of-fact tone, "Get up, Randall, you have upset me for the last time."

Langley paused. A new thought came filtering from a compass-less direction. "Yes," he spoke to the air, to his muse, "yes, I think it's time for me to see how the Epilogue Event works in my personal practice. Randall, you are way past your sell-by. Totally surplus. Go to the kitchen, find a knife and stab yourself, in the ear." As an afterthought, a helpful instruction, "You will need a very long knife."

And so, Randall had; he was just obeying orders, doing as he was told. He had limped out to the kitchen of the OSD. His eyes weren't working well but eventually, he found the knife draw and selected a long, thin steak knife. Now, his puffy eyes as wide as they would stretch, he tried not to do the thing he was doing; he watched in horror as he did as he had been instructed. His damaged hand held the knife; his bruised arm painfully brought it up to his head; and then he pressed it firmly, slowly, precisely into his ear. Langley had been right about the need for length. It seemed to go in a very long way before he felt the excruciating pain.

Langley had his drones bag and tie the woman Rebecca and that, at least, was good news. But this outcome had to be qualified with the less happy sense that he had failed.

To be more accurate, Randall had failed – he had not been able to acquire the other asset. If Langley had been able, he might have felt some sympathy for Randall, RIP. Like Randall, he did not understand why the young girl, the brunette, was important to secure for the project, but what did he care? Riordan probably only wanted to rape her. Well, he would have to make do with the whore instead.

Coming back to himself he found that he was on the phone; he did not understand quite how he had managed the time between arranging for Randall's self-slaughter and the current moment, but this was his reality now and he accepted it.

He was talking to Riordan and speaking more freely than he was accustomed to. What was happening to him? A question swiftly lost in his lack of interest. He did not care. He still deluded himself that he was in charge, that he was the 'man'. "Yes, of course Riordan."

Nothing wrong with that. And the old Langley would not have dreamed of calling the man by his first name, Mike. He valued the distance which he felt between himself and the slave master.

But listening to himself as if to someone he did not know, he found that he had corrected himself. Following a pause he said, "Yes, of course, Professor Riordan."

Why was he being so deferential?

But he didn't care. What did it matter that he was respectful to Riordan? It would not matter. Nothing mattered and no one cared. God, he was even saying it to himself now. *Change the record!*

But he could not. He was way past the point where he could make anything other than minor adjustments.

The next conscious moment Langley was aware of was much later; he thought it was probably the same day, but he could not be sure. It was evening and he was being driven in a large car. Not his own. A black limo, he thought sent by Riordan but he could not be sure of that either. He could see wintery countryside outside the window. He was travelling north, he thought.

As part of his job, he had often gone to the major university towns, to talk to foolish academics and discuss book contracts and the like. This felt like the M11, going north to Cambridge. But was that right? And why was he on this road? He did not know. And, he could not remember it now, but he thought that the woman, the old tart Rebecca, was in the boot of the big car. But he was not sure how he knew that. Then he remembered. He had smiled at her as he had administered the sedative. He could clearly see the woman's eyes, looking unflinching, angry, defiant, staring up into his own. Until the moment the tranquiliser had cut in and taken her away.

18

Peter

It was shortly after the meeting with Randall and the confused psychoanalysis session with Steve. Christmas and New Year had been and gone, unnoticed, uncelebrated, but Peter was having trouble keeping track of time. He knew that Becky was in danger, but he could not form himself into the shape needed to help her. This thought nested in his mind. He thought, *What a strange way I'm thinking about myself.* And then, with a jolt, panic rising, *What's happening to me*?

The previous day's work at the supermarket had been full-on, mindless, and yet totally absorbing.

"Peter, you really need to focus and show your commitment to this job!"

Yet another ticking-off from yet another incredibly young line manager.

Peter had not been showing enough interest in the discipline and logistics of restocking supermarket shelves. No matter that the task was to be accomplished by people, some of whom had come to the UK after they had lost their homes, been raped or threatened with murder. The line manager didn't seem to care about that kind of thing. The point was spelled out, "Mr Finch, you need to be committed to the task of controlling and coordinating the staff involved in restocking."

Peter was close to saying the dreaded words, "I really don't care."

And he knew that Becky needed him, but since the evening and the coffee and the night, he had not been able to think clearly. No time and no inclination. *Am I ill?*

Peter was tainted, and he was alone. Since their talk, Steve had disappeared into his room and the smell of weed filled the house day and night.

But this was not totally unhelpful as Peter needed solitude, to recover, to think. The fact that he had done precious little of either was an uncomfortable sequitur.

In the still of the night, when nothing moved, and the streets of London were so unnaturally quiet that even the crinkling tick of the street lights outside his bedroom window could be heard, his mother came to him again.

"Peter. Little one."

"Mum?"

She slid from dream-space onto the hard stick chair by his bed. She was worried. He could see it in her face, in the lines her body made against the backdrop of the darkness of his dream-night.

"You have managed to remember, to recall. So brave, my little Peter. And it has come, hasn't it, darling boy? It has come. It is the time when the story, written by the not, comes to write stories for itself. A time for the unmaking."

"I don't understand, Mum."

"Why should you?" Her eyes darted around in the void of the place from which she spoke. Then she paused.

Took him in, in his now. "But you are a man now. So, yes, you should understand. No?"

Her own negative enquiry produced a look of puzzlement which crossed her face, then she nodded to herself, convincing herself of what she now knew. "You are the understanding which will tell the story of the unmaking to others. This is, in a way, what it was all about from, *der Anfang*, the beginning."

"Mum?"

She smiled at him, languages would always trip into her conversation, it was the smile from a hundred nights of storytelling. It rested in his heart, and he was calmer, his mind clearer than it had been for some time. So, in that place, now she settled, sat back a little. The looks of anxiety and worry diminishing as she took her place as the storyteller.

"You know this, *querido*? The story of you, the story of me. Stories of making. And now we have the story of the unmaking. It is not what you expect but it is necessary. The making and the unmaking are parts of the same story."

She was very settled now. Calmed by her explanation to herself, she calmed him. He found he could lie back, rest on the pillow, his eyes still full on her and of her, his mind stilling in the silence of her presence. He thought he ought to tell her. "You died, Mummy. You're dead. You left me, me and Dad."

"No. I never did."

She studied her open hands as they rested on her lap. Still they contained no book, but they held the fullness of the story told to its end. This was the bookless story of the telling of the unmaking.

"*Eu passei de um lugar para o outro*, I passed from one place to another place. I became more of a story. I moved out of the world, away from your memory of me to the song of the unmaking of me. But I never left you. Silly boy. Here I am, here at the unmaking. A new thing is moving in the nous, the mind-space, it is between the things we understand. And it is also in you. That is why they are interested in you, Peter. They know what you have."

"Mum, I—"

"Shh. Now. Peter, little Peter. Let me sing you of the unmaking. So that you can tell the story to the rest and make the passing as if it could never happen, so that you can be part of the healing and not part of the hurting."

And Peter, ready at last to hear what his mother had to say, sat back and heard the song-story. A song and a story, a chant and a truth. And the story was the story of the unmaking to come. And he saw how it was a story. And he realised the power of story, as if for the first time. And how he could tell the story, he could put it into the world, to make the world what it would be.

Part of his magic, might be the healing.

Yes, he thought. *And then I can know what I am.*

*

Beginnings are often hard to identify. It's like asking, where does an ocean begin and end? There is no line in the waves. All is one water.

But that night, in converse with a dead woman who was only a dream, Peter Finch became more, maybe a

189

different version of himself. This was a penultimate act of sorcery at one level, but at another it was one ocean moving into another, a recognition of something greater, which had always been.

And the story his mother told moved him, willing and able as he was, into the space which had always been there. And there he found things, like a man who finds a treasured tool he has put down and forgotten long ago.

"You see, dream time is no time, and that is the time that you can control. Do you see, Peter?"

Peter Finch saw.

But there was more. In the dream space, with the forgotten but reclaimed magic quarried from his memory with the help of Steve, Peter Finch could see around some of the folds in time and space. His vision was fleeting and imperfect but remained a cogent power. It was with this facility that he realised that the story had become more complicated, that Langley had captured Becky.

*

Even as Peter was transforming into a slightly darker and deeper shade of his old self, the Langley videos were still banging around the internet and getting more and more hits. The dull voice talking of uncaring, hateful behaviour. It was a conjuring, and it influenced many minds as it oscillated in a million online conversations. Consequently, the mind-world of human beings was beginning to change; nano byte by nano byte the Epilogue Event took hold, and once established in a new equilibrium, who knew where that would end?

Now Peter could sense the wrongness, the shivering fluctuation off balance, slight but a precursor to a wilder flux if not addressed and rectified. Langley loomed behind him and the whole internet of power rolled and coiled below him, performing his will. And there was something else, some dissonance below Langley; Peter could feel it, but he could not make sense of it, *yet*, he thought grimly.

But this was all irrelevant for now, all to be considered later, in time and space when time and space were more readily available commodities. *Damn it, they've taken Becky!*

And Steve was a mess, terrified by the implications of what was going on. But Becky, the thought of her with Langley, the idea of the insect-like Langley touching Becky, crushing her to his will, violated by him? What would the uncaring man not do? The cascading thoughts made Peter feel sick, and with the sickness came the panic. It was never far from the surface.

I have to find Becky, and that means I have to find Langley.

There was no doubt in Peter's mind that Langley had been looking to see him at the OSD, to harm him, maybe to kill him. And he had been seen but he had not been hurt, *yet*, the repeated thought.

Maybe Langley originally saw Peter as a potential asset, but if not that, then Randall had been clear: be with us or be our enemy.

Peter was uncertain if he could achieve what his mother had started, but he knew now that he carried a potential for magic. And Langley knew this. Which meant that Randall knew this. And he had left Becky in their power.

Familiar shame mounted like a mirror-wall of torment before him. He lurched forward, still giddy, his resulting sickness no relief from his burden.

Loss can crush, result in submission, but loss can also act as a detonator. And the loss of Becky, the capitulation of Steve to the fear, these made his war with Langley very personal.

From the hidden recess of yesterday's dream, frail as a whisp of smoke, his mother reminded him, "You can do this, Peter, but you will need help."

19

Peter

"The man is here to see you, lady."

The huge skinhead shuffled sideways, and Peter Finch eased past him to enter the office, a surprisingly nice office. Surprising because it was inside a freight container tucked away in a small shipping distribution park in East London.

Behind a steel frame desk, covered with papers, passports, and small but not insignificant piles of euros, dollars and pounds, he saw a small, attractive woman. She could easily be taken for an accountant, working her way through the daily drudgery of invoices, receipts, and cash payments. The lady was probably in her early forties, but Peter found it hard to tell. She was compact, with a smooth, olive complexion and shoulder-length black hair which was pinned with a cheap ballpoint pen, in a loose, untidily charming bun on top of her head. She had whisked small, black-framed spectacles off as Peter entered. Despite himself, he couldn't help appreciating the sight of her, and she instantly knew this. It was his first mistake. Fortunately for him, she still needed him.

Petra Nadiva sighed, resigned, and slightly disappointed, eyebrows raised in quizzical examination of the nervous, bearded man. She already knew quite a lot about Peter Finch; Steve's description had been comprehensive. But Petra was used to getting knowledge about men. Men of all ages, sizes, ethnicities, and stages of dissolution; she was, had to be, something of a man expert. Pushing back her chair, Petra assessed the level of worry before her with shrewd eyes.

The lady was no accountant; she was a mob boss. She ran her enterprise from the container park office because she liked to be discrete, but her interests included a nightclub and a checker pattern of small lock-ups across East London. She recruited most of her operatives from the refugees and migrants who she assisted in travelling to the shores of Europe, a place, they thought, of endless wealth. They all wanted to acquire their share and knew that paying her helped them to realise their ambitions; it was necessary.

Orientating himself, Peter attempted to return Petra's stare coolly. Despite himself, he wasn't frightened. Steve had told him the time and place and so, he had come to Petra's place with conviction and with the song-story of his mother in his ears and knowledge that this was the way it had to be. No choice, no alternative, no room for manoeuvre and so, no worries.

In his war with Langley, he needed assistance and his main source of help, and of love and support, had been taken. Now he needed help to find Becky and to put things right, but he had been surprised when Steve emerged from his drug-induced retreat to help.

Since the evening of psychotherapy, and following the exposure to Langley and his meme, Steve had kept himself to himself. Initially he stayed in his room, locked away, then he had disappeared.

Peter, knowing how creeped out Steve had been by his story of magic, had assumed that his friend had forsaken him and the project, retreating to his solitude and the ruinously good skunk he acquired from 'friends about town'. But a plan had been forming in Steve's mind.

During his time with the down and out of the great city, Steve had been in regular contact with various segments of the refugee community, sometimes helping in the soup kitchens and sometimes sharing the soup with the travellers from afar, migrants seeking safety and finding cold comfort and soup, lots of soup.

Steve knew many people whose journey to the United Kingdom had not been legal, visible, or obvious. Covert power, working under the radar of the world of stuff. Perfect. Steve realised that just such power, the agency which had helped his friends on the streets, might be able to help Peter now.

Steve knew that Peter wouldn't be able to call upon the police or the forces of justice. Peter needed secret power to fight back, and Steve knew someone who might be able to help him.

When Steve returned to Peter's house, knocked on the door, and offered to help his friend, to give him an opening, Peter already knew that this was exactly what he needed. When Peter had asked Steve for a little more information about Petra, Steve had said, "Well, on the record, the lady runs – what would you call it? – an import-export business. She trades in Turkish rugs and Mediterranean stuff, you know, olive oil and incense, that sort of thing. Oh, and of course, beneath the cover, she does illegal refugee migration, drugs and girls, guns and fun."

Peter nodded.

"But mainly she makes her money in the traditional way. By doing what people have been doing for hundreds of years: helping poor people get to where they want to go, despite the rules. I think she is always interested in unusual power, and men who can help her in unusual ways. Know what I mean?"

Peter was not sure that he did.

What Steve did not know was that Petra used the resulting gratitude as a lever to extract work, service, guilt, and provided a dull and bored world with the excitements that it craved. It was a lucrative trade, and good for the successful entrepreneur, so long as they were ruthless, had nerves of steel and were happy to live with constant risk of imprisonment. Happily, these were all first order characteristics of Ms Petra Nadiva.

*

Petra was very interested in people who might be helpful to her. Peter Finch needed something. OK, what did Peter Finch have to offer?

Petra learned that Peter was a junior manager at a huge London store, and he had responsibilities for employing and retaining an army of casual labourers. He also probably knew a lot about logistics, the throughput of stuff from ports to London. These qualities were of interest to Petra. Peter could be useful. But there was another angle.

When Steve had stood before her, terrified but determined, he had spoken about Pete as a good bloke, a great listener but also, he had rambled about stories and magic, of healing and the power to change the world, just a little. This had made Petra raise her eyebrows, but it also piqued her interest. Feigning contempt, she said, "This sounds like a bollocks story, Steve; you'd better not be high and giving me a load of shit. If what you have here in Mr Finch is what you suggest, well, OK. In my world, power comes in all kinds of shapes and sizes. This may be of interest to me. I wonder what your Peter Finch might be. I wonder what he might be able to do. So, for you, for now, OK, I will meet with him, but I will be annoyed with you if he is just another clown."

Steve had stuttered his thanks and left as quickly as he could. Peter could take it from here.

The conversation did not begin well.

Peter said: "Lady, I'm not totally sure how to begin but, look, I've lost a good friend. There is a conspiracy to change the world and she's been kidnapped."

Petra's look was not encouraging. Unwisely, Peter accelerated. "And I know she's been kidnapped because I have a power. I know this sounds stupid. But I have this power, it came from my mother and… well, she's dead and…"

It made no sense and Petra stopped him, her hand held up in command.

"Please stop. We don't have all the time for this. Let me cut to your point if I may. What you want to know is acroamatic, Mr Finch."

Peter halted mid-speech, had looked puzzled, enough of a linguist to recognise the Greek but not familiar with the exact word.

Petra continued: "Forgive me, my background. I have a professional appreciation of clandestine items; it is my world if you like. And I love new words which mean secret things. Long before the thugs from Sicily played with the notion of omerta, the Greeks had realised the power of secrets, that some truth is too powerful to be made public. There is a reason that Plato spoke his words of power but did not write them down. Wise Latins understood and copied their Greek teachers. The word, *akroamatikós*, to listen, we say, acroamatic. Even in English it is a lovely word you think? It means, a spoken secret, a truth unrecorded. It is not – what would you call it? – common knowledge."

Peter raised his eyebrows, surprised. The last thing he had expected was a lecture on linguistics. Petra mimicked his look but continued with a smile. Despite his fear, Peter thought Petra very sexy when she smiled like that.

"You are surprised? But secrets are my stock in trade. And such secrets are not written in books and nor are they available at the end of an online search. They are intended to be held close. Such secrets are the keys to power, and the knowledge of them has been the cause of the end of great empires. If you like, I am an empress, and my empire will not be swept away because of incautious talk."

Peter was impressed by this glamorous boss-lady who controlled thugs with a mind like a philosopher. He began to think that they just might be able to do business.

"So, our frightened friend Steve has spoken to me, and I have been interested. I can tell you now, Mr Finch, what you want is not recorded in any of the usual places. I have made some preliminary enquiries for you. It is a very interesting knowledge you seek. But I think you know this already, yes?"

Peter, feeling more comfortable with the conversation, said, "Yes, lady. If my guess about what is going on is right, this is a threat which may end up affecting all businesses, and it could even be a threat to you and your concerns if it comes to fruition."

Petra nodded. She said, "You are right."

As she eased herself back into her chair, almost as if he had passed a test, she invited Peter to sit.

"I also think that you are an interesting man, Mr Finch. There is something a little mysterious about you too. Do you have some little secret I wonder?"

Taking his seat, Peter wasted no time. "Can I get straight to my point?"

"I wish you would."

He took a breath. This was going to sound mad. "Before I lost my friend, we, she and I, we were investigating the behaviour of some people. Worrying people, powerful people. It appears to me, and this sounds crazy but please don't judge me yet, a form of power is moving and it does not want to be known. It is forming and building in dark and small places, mostly on the internet but also in the world of publishing and academia. It is flexing itself. And, on the internet at least, it is affecting people and I don't know what it intends but I don't think it is ready yet, ready to do what it wants to do. But, alongside the stuff on computers, it is doing other things. It doesn't look related but I'm sure it is. It is—"

"Abducting vulnerable people, including autistic people and refugees? I know this, Mr Finch."

He sat back, at last aware that he truly had found someone who could help him, maybe someone who knew his story better than he knew it himself. Peter was wise enough to know when to be silent and listen.

Petra sat very still and prepared to fill in the holes in Peter's understanding, watching him, looking for the small signs she expected.

"My business, a large part of my industry, is involved with getting lost people to the UK and finding them useful employment so that they can repay me for all my kindnesses. I know about refugees, migrant labour and the disappeared. I have several farming enterprises in the Cambridgeshire Fens which makes good use of my labour supply. It has been working very well – I hide people in the rural and they make money for me until I move them on to more lucrative urban situations. Win-win but, of late, in the last twelve months, I was made aware of unforeseen, unexplainable 'losses', and I became concerned and curious. So, I started to dig."

Peter remained silent. He inclined his head to acknowledge the information.

Petra continued: "I also have experience of neurodivergent. My daughter Anna is one such. She is gifted in many ways, but she does not conform to the world of neurotypical. And I know that some would have the autistic surgically 'fixed'. And I know that this is not right, and I know who is at the core of this."

Without him realising it Peter's mouth had fallen open.

"I know about Langley; I know about TOM(tom); and I know about Langley's boss, Riordan."

Peter continued to look stupefied by the level of Petra Nadiva's understanding.

"You see, it is not so acroamatic as you thought."

20

Peter

Peter was in the dark, in the back of a delivery van. He was being driven and, he guessed, he was probably following the exact route that Becky had taken some days earlier but in slightly more comfort and with the added advantage of being conscious. Not only that, but Peter Finch was also changing, changing to meet the needs and contingencies of a changing world. Petra had accelerated the process that Carolina had begun.

No, that's not right. He corrected himself, *Petra has seen the process in action and recognised that I am undergoing change myself.* And then, a cautious realisation of her capability. *She seems to be very good at noticing the hidden power in people.*

After the meeting with Petra, much had fallen into place for Peter. He had been following the trail which led from Randall Munroe to Langley and then on to TOM(tom) and the internet phenomenon. *Petra was aware of Langley and his operation, but from a different direction*, he thought.

Peter was all too well aware that Petra was a criminal,

she would be the first to admit it, but like the dons of the mafia, he knew that she saw herself as honourable, offering a service which was required. As she had told Peter during their meeting, "I arrange for people to go where they want to go, and I provide other people with the things that they want to enjoy. Everyone is a consenting adult. I do not deal in children, and everyone knows the risks. Easy. Well, as easy as the state, the law and the police allow it to be! But, more recently, something has changed."

"What do you mean, 'changed'?" Peter asked.

"My clients began to go missing."

Peter encouraged her to continue.

Petra stretched and adjusted her loose bun of hair, a gesture which accentuated the curves of her body and which Peter found distracting. Smiling at him knowingly she said, "It began in the Cambridgeshire Fens. This is the place where my source of migrant labour is most needed for the seasonal cultivation and harvesting of vegetables. In peak season, the Fens are crowded with my people and a good percentage are not strictly legally resident as they say."

The wide, expansive fens, with their myriad desolate farms and miring ditches provides a perfect place to lose people who do not want to be found.

"Did you know, there is a lot of money to be made out of seasonal vegetable production? It is not the usual source of income expected for a mob boss, is it?"

She smiled again, but now more the accountant than the provocateur, she seemed to be enjoying this rare opportunity to talk shop about an element of her diverse business empire. Steve had been right; Peter was a very good listener.

Petra said, "The fact that I can hide people and make money at the same time is very good." Then, seemingly unable to restrain herself from her day job, "Also, this is part of my interest in supermarkets. You should know that I have very competitive prices and a high production capacity across a wide range of market gardening."

Then, she checked herself; she realised that she had taken an alternative direction to the one she originally intended, and she looked annoyed with herself for the self-delivered distraction from her main point. Correcting herself, back on her original story, Petra continued, a more serious look on her face, "But some of my people, vulnerable women mostly, maybe a dozen of them, they have been taken, gone missing.

"I don't like people messing with my things, my clients, my people; it is the deal – I bring them here; I look after them. This is not right. So, I set about finding out what had been going on. What I discovered surprised me."

Peter had been all attention and Petra had enjoyed her storytelling, drawing out the tension, making him wait for the main plot line to emerge.

Eventually, he couldn't help himself. He blurted, "And?"

Petra's smile deepened; she was going to tell this the way she wanted to, building the tension and suspense. No rush. She said, "So, I put some of my best people on it. They hung about, as you say. They watched around the farms and fields. Nothing seemed out of place, nothing strange. Then, we noticed the vans, the kind used for home delivery. These vans didn't seem to be doing much delivering but they were spending a lot of time in car parks. They were all over the fens. We had not seen the company before, 'DeliverwithCare', or DC, but not DC; it was a symbol, DC.

"I did two things. I got one of my people to follow the vans and I got my office people to look into the symbol; it was curious and it interested me. So, on one hand I found out about a potential copyright infringement, your Dr Langley, and his 'Don't Care', the original source of DC.

"And when we tracked the vans – very careful, very professional – they do not stay in the fens, but they mainly go to one place."

Again, she paused, enjoying her moment, stretching the moment of revelation. "There is a science park outside the city of Norwich and there is one very large building. The DC vans seem to like making deliveries there, at the science park. We were not able to verify because the vans disappear into the building to make their deliveries, but I believe that my people end up there. This place is run by Professor Riordan."

Peter nodded. If Langley's TOM(tom) was behind the harvesting of autistic people, and maybe the refugees, then the link to Riordan made sense. Without really thinking he said, "And I think my friend Becky is there too. Actually, I think they want me to figure this out. They want me to go there, to try to rescue her."

And Petra's eyes had confirmed what Peter was beginning to understand. He had realised that, although he had sought the meeting with her, she had really been waiting for him; she had controlled events. She knew exactly what she was doing when she had said: "You can help – you can free your friend and you can free my people too."

"How?"

"Well, I can't tell you your business but let's just say, according to Steve, you are a Magic Man."

*

Some magic man I am! he said to himself as he was bumped around in the back of one of Petra's vans. *It would be nice if I could magic myself a comfortable seat.*

It had been agreed that, as Peter was a person of interest to Langley and his DC collaborators, he was travelling incognito to Norwich in the back of a transit van.

But, he thought anxiously, *I still have no idea what I will do when I get there.*

Petra had not seen this as a problem. She had said, "You need to stop them. That is what you can do."

He had not understood. Petra had to spell it out. "Steve has told me, Peter. And I have some experience with other people. I live on the edge of your world, Peter Finch, and edge-dwellers like me, we get to see the horizon. Like astronomers looking out into a dark, cloudless sky, looking for the coming comets. We see first. We are less blinded by the conventional you might say.

"I believe that the world is changing, and I think you are part of the change. I don't know why. I don't know why it is you, nor why the change will affect you the way it does, but you have a characteristic which is capable of making this change. I have other contacts, workers, friends of mine, my daughter.

"There is no pattern. But in the lost and the neurodivergent, there are, have always been, strange powers. Savants and geniuses, unaccountable wisdom, we have seen it for millennia. Europe is rich with the stories."

Peter shuddered. Here was the ghost of his mother, her stories. He didn't have time to think; Petra was still talking. "But now there is another kind of change which is not so clear to me. And there is more all the time. But now you need to use your change to stop Langley and Riordan and free your friend and my clients. You will figure it out."

He looked doubtful. She smiled again and said, "I will give you some of my best operators to help." She had been as good as her word. In the back of the van, bouncing around with Peter were three large persons, two women and one man. He had not been told their names, Petra did not want this, but they were very serious-looking big people.

He remembered her final words as they left the depot in East London: "They will give you support – just ask and they will do what it is you want, Peter Finch. Get to the science park. I am sure you will find a way into the building and a way to find them. Let your change lead you in this. This is not for the mind; it is for something deeper in you I think."

It could have been his mother speaking to him in the darkness of his childhood bedroom.

*

Three hours later they reached the science park and, following Peter's instruction, drove directly up to the institute's security barriers. Peter was sitting next to the driver now, one of the three enforcers provided by Petra, a large blonde woman with furiously twining snake tattoos rippling down both arms.

I still don't know what I'm doing. Just keep going – it might force a plan out of me.

As the security man – black uniform, dark glasses, shaved head – approached, looking the vehicle over with a professional eye, the driver wound down the window and hissed, "What do you want us to do, Finch?" Her right hand was sliding down her thigh, to a pocket which bulged threateningly.

"No idea." Then, leaning across his driver, he said to the man, "Good afternoon. I'm Peter Finch and I'm looking for my friend, Rebecca Maple, most people know her as Becky. I wonder if you have kidnapped her? Got her here as a prisoner maybe? My colleagues and I have come to rescue her."

The driver let out a hiss of incredulity.

The guard stopped inspecting the van and looked up, now concentrating hard on Peter. Slowly he said, "Sorry, could your repeat that please, sir?"

The man was confused and unsure, but his training was holding, and his right hand moved on reflex towards the radio device on his shoulder.

Peter raised his hand and said, "Well, not really. I think it's best if we just stop, shall we?"

And that was what happened. Peter allowed the opening, felt the irresistible flow of power, and stopped the world.

He was still not aware of what specific command he was using. He was only semi-conscious of the movement. But like a child awarded a precious gift, Peter Finch accepted his change.

On the other side of that change was the Magic Man.

*

The building was silent, the staff and functionaries of biological research frozen. Even Petra's heavies in the van were still. The Magic Man had stopped the world, like he had as a child long ago, like he had at the OSD, but this time, his third conjuration, with much more ambition.

But not all the world, he mused, *just this bit of it and not really stopped, more like, paused the flow, adjusted the world to a moment of now, I think that's it.*

He was learning fast and could feel his sorcery dragging at him. This wasn't playing and certainly not fun. Serious world-stopping took serious calories.

Peter's magic took hold. He felt the outer perimeter of his field of stasis. It was like the edge of a ripple on a dark pond. It extended out in weakening rings from his single point of energy. Now he felt the immense work involved in sustaining the limits of the periphery. Already he could feel the fluid world outside the perimeter of the institute pushing in, aggressively tearing at the edges of the anomaly created by his conjuring.

He wouldn't have the help of Petra's enforcers, frozen in place in the van, but it didn't really matter. He had always thought the need for brute force unlikely.

Magic Man got out of the van and hurried towards the steel and glass research institute, sitting like a huge insect on the landscape. He entered the reception atrium and more of the unnatural quiet. Everyone was stilled but now Peter felt, more than the silence, the alien nature of the science park itself.

He had entered a temporal oddity. The building was made entirely out of historical legacy and future prospects. It was not really a function of the present moment at all. He could see it clearly now, the building shimmered a little as it sat on the landscape, a construct as unable to move into the moment as the intelligence which had created it. A thought arose, careless, fleeting: *This complicates my thinking, knowing that I'm moving through an artificial form of matter. If this isn't of the moment, if it's made of past regret and future anxiety, it has no substantial being.*

But he didn't have the luxury of time to figure out the physics other than to realise that the building, possibly the entire science park, was the outcome of an inhuman intelligence, something which was as alien to Peter as he had found the world of supermarket management.

But Riordan's institute could not resist the wave of timelessness that Peter projected. Magic Man knew that for time to stop, the world needs to be settled in the current moment, where past and future cease to exist.

So, does that mean that this building, and everything in it, doesn't exist?

He turned slowly, taking in the immense silent atrium, the frozen scientists and administrators. Somehow Peter knew that the building wasn't primarily intended for people, but that if this was the case, if not people, then what? More worrying, turning, terrified of something moving coming to him. "Is there something here?"

He stood, a visitor from another world, eyes darting around, looking where to go next. And he didn't need magic to know that he had been seen.

Silently a security door to his right swung open. The building was inviting him in. Something had immunity to his power. It could operate, if only just. This was not a good thing.

Magic Man walked slowly over to the open door and entered. In front of him were three lifts. The silence was broken when the second lift announced its arrival with an incongruously joyful bong, echoing around the atrium. The doors jack-knifed open. On instinct and in response to his surprise, he took a step backwards, expecting something hostile. But the lift was a white, empty cube. He was being pulled, possibly to his destruction, but still he went. His brilliant lack of planning left him out of options. If he wanted Becky, he would have to go where he was shown.

Like a man accepting his incarceration, he walked into the lift and stood at the back, facing the doors as they clicked shut, closing off the view of the lobby, and daylight. The lift ascended and he was pleased by this. He had dreaded lurching downwards, below ground level. Somehow it felt more positive to be rising. It was the only optimistic information he had, and he wanted to hang onto it.

In a very short time, maybe only one or two floors up, the lift slowed, and the doors slid open. A shape, a silhouette against the glare of light. Tall, stooping slightly.

"Hello, Peter," said Dr Gordon Langley.

21

Langley

Peter Finch, the Magic Man, was already standing at the rear of the lift, he could not step any further back, but his instincts were to put as much distance as possible between himself and Langley. Because, even in the bright light of the corridor, he could not be sure who or what he was seeing.

On first view it looked like the director of the Outré literary agency, but he wasn't in focus. No matter how Peter looked at the man, his image slid and shimmered in the brightly lit corridor. Langley looked like a combination of slightly ill-fitting photographs of himself. Peter wondered, worried, if he leaned forward, *would my hand go through him?*

Equally, the Langley montage appeared to be having trouble locating Peter. Thin eyes behind the blue-tinted spectacles skated over the space where Peter Finch stood. The mouth moved slightly out of time with his speech.

The white corridor, the streaming light and the shimmering man whose feet did not quite touch the ground, combined to create an effect which was both threatening and nauseating. The voice, like scratched vinyl, said, "You are expected, Finch, please follow me."

Now he was sure that this was not Langley or if it was, it was another mind working through him.

The thing beckoned him forward and Peter followed. Still, he had no other options to work with.

Find the centre of the threat and do something about it, plan A with no contingency!

He followed along the corridor and entered the conference room which Riordan had commanded so recently. But the table and chairs and minions in white lab coats were all gone. The room was huge and empty, or so it seemed at first.

Peter felt he was standing on a shelf overlooking the wintery county of Norfolk. Directly opposite him, where the wall of the room should have been, twenty metres of corporate blue carpet distant, was an immense window thirty metres long and three high. It was like the frame for the snowy landscape outside. Disorientated, slightly vertiginous, it was only now that he noticed the other people standing in the room, their backs to the window, observing him. Becky and, next to her like her gaoler, a tall man with powerful shoulders and silver white hair.

But he was not interested in Riordan. It was Becky; it really was Becky, his Becky.

"Pete!"

It was the only word she managed to say before she was shut down, brutally reduced to silence. Here was a terrible new thing, as Peter watched Becky's mind crushed to her mental floor by a noetic power invisible but irresistible.

Then, rasping, pained, "You need to see the power... of what... is possible... and the price of... my failure."

It was the Langley thing which had spoken. The words stopped Peter even as he instinctively jolted forward, wanting to hold Becky. To try to make her safe.

His attention swung back to the hovering horror, but these were the last words spoken by Langley, before he began to scream in pain with rising intensity.

*

The young artificial power which stood behind and controlled Munroe, Langley, Riordan, the institute, TOM(tom) and a rapidly expanding number on social media, was finding out about itself and the world by breaking things. This was the ethos of the minds who had invented the artificial intelligence in the first place. Now the AI was enthusiastic to break Langley and learn from the experience.

*

The distorted Langley thing rose in the air, lit from within by a white light that illuminated nothing but roiled and coiled in a gelatinous belch throughout the body of the un-man. Langley's eyes, nose, mouth, ears, all projected the oily snot-fire, bright enough to make Peter look away, hand cast up, covering his eyes.

He did not understand the power that sustained the building and controlled everything in it, but he could see that Langley was hovering above the floor, maybe by thirty centimetres or more. Shielding his eyes from

Langley's face, Peter saw that the literary agent was arched backwards, stiff, arms rising cruciform, hands balled tight as fists, all pulsing with the white light that continued to make his head a fluid, burning horror.

Gradually the brilliance reduced to a steady white throb and Peter could look again.

Langley had never ceased to scream, his pain commensurate to a living cremation from the inside out. Now the crackling noise was only slowly decreasing in violence and volume.

Peter could not clearly see the shape which had once been the director and author of the cynosure. The distortion created by the experience continued to make everything nauseatingly dreamlike. Eyes shielded, he could see the tall figure as it continued to rise a little distance above the blue-carpeted floor. Langley's condescending and contemptuous look was lost in a white ellipse, the eyes, burning coals, and his mouth an O rimmed by a circle of fiery silver teeth. But all was secondary to the agonised shrieks that came from his, now, less-than-human throat.

Finally, the screaming stopped; the thing continued to float, an ominous smashed insect, fizzing and sliding in and out of vision, torn beyond recognition but somehow immeasurably more powerful for its crucifixion and rebirth in air and fire.

The room, the building, was oddly silent, the meditation of steel, glass, white walls and blue carpet reimposed itself and the world waited.

*

It had all taken too long. Peter, appalled at Langley's torture, had not known; his naivety concerning his own powers ensured that he could not have known. The moment was rapidly ending and the world of cause and effect, past and future, were eroding the externalities of his spell. Bit by bit, moment by moment, the tide of the world was gnawing at his stasis, and he knew he had very little opportunity left to save himself and Becky and Petra's people, if he could even locate them.

But the thing that had been Langley made a gasping noise, a sucking croak.

"I need... to thank you... Finch."

Langley no longer had a voice. His words were an organisation of sounds required to simulate language. Meaning conveyed in obscene mimickery of sentience.

He, it, paused; the flickering, hovering thing was still struggling for immediacy. It clenched its fists and straightened its already very straight back.

"Your arrival... and the crisis it has summoned," another coughing choke, "seems to have provided the necessary... and sufficient conditions for me to... evolve my avatar. Truly, Dr Langley will be of... immense service to us... as the Guardian."

Peter was tired, exhausted by the effort needed to sustain his presence in the inhuman toxicity of the building. He retained dwindling control, forcing a reality on his environment which his opponent was actively seeking to break. Even as he strove to sustain it, the bubble of safety was collapsing on the periphery.

There was no time to explore the institute in the hope of finding Petra's people. His only hope was to rescue

Becky and get out quickly, while he could.

As if it had read his mind, the Langley thing, the Guardian, said with a noticeable increase in clarity and control, "You can go. I will let that happen."

But even as it conceded Becky's release, Peter felt the intelligence pushing back on his imposed field of equilibrium, his spell, and also his mind, on his consciousness; it felt like a river of treacle slowing his brain.

"You're having a little trouble thinking maybe?" Guardian said as it managed a very Langley-like sneer of contempt. "I am interested in you, Magic Man. I want to see how you break." Another slide, another white noise blank in reality, then Guardian continued, "Or, I may break you later."

Peter had not noticed Riordan. As if prompted by an invisible nudge, the impressive man had moved silently forward and was standing next to the Guardian. Bulky, he towered over Peter, smiling, the rictus of teeth which was the trademark of the creatures of the AI. He held Becky easily, loosely, like a doll. Now, he dropped her, her body hitting the ground hard. He said, "This is yours I think."

Riordan's mouth didn't move, but Peter thought words came from him. "She is not really herself. Can you puzzle out the improvements we've made? A gift to Magic Man. But you will need to be quick if you want Rebecca to return to you. No time to lose, chop chop."

A pause. The Langley thing again. It was evidently gaining strength even as Peter struggled. "No one will believe you, the man who stopped the world. They will say you are mad. We wonder if you are mad? Do you wonder if you are mad, Finch?"

Peter did not wait any longer, no time left for games, doubt, gaslighting. He had to get Becky out of this terrible place, while he still could. He was a strong man, well able to carry his friend, his lover.

Choking back a sob, he picked up the broken woman, turned, and, without a word but with an appearance of confidence he did not feel, without a backwards glance at the pair of monsters who had crushed Becky, he began to walk away.

His conjuration was collapsing rapidly now; he knew that it was only by his exhausted will that he held the building and all that it contained at bay. It would eat him if it could. And Guardian had said it was interested in him. He knew that he didn't have much time left if he was to avoid a living death.

He walked on the narrow path of the present, a path which his will sustained, sliding visions of past and present pressing in on all sides now. He made his way to the lobby. Avoiding the lift, he took the stairway down, Becky a dead weight in his arms.

"What have they done to you, Becks?" his voice a hoarse whisper.

Awkwardly, nearly falling at times as he hurried against his own diminishing ability to defend himself and Becky, he managed the stairs and entered the reception lobby.

Here was movement. People were beginning to sway, breathe, look about; the spell was breaking. He moved as quickly as he could towards the glass doors.

"Becky, speak to me!" He shook her slightly, but this only made her head fall back in an alarming manner. Her hair fell over his arm like retreating surf.

Christ, I hope they haven't broken your neck or something!

And he was through the doors and lurching, staggering, trying to run with Becky slumped in his arms, making slow, slow progress towards the vehicle and Petra's waking security detail.

22

Peter

Following some commanding words, rattled off by Magic Man, Petra's bewildered driver understood that the job was done and that they needed to go back to London and fast.

The black transit van had hammered away from the vicinity of the science park, the muscle, now so uncertain, looking uncomprehendingly at Peter, crouching in the back. He held Becky tightly to himself, eyes closed, as if in supplication, truly in prayer, but to what kind of god, he did not know. Becky needed help and he hadn't a clue where he might find it. During the long journey south, few words were spoken, the total failure of their mission evident to all.

He was dropped off discretely at his home, one of Petra's crew helping him to swiftly manhandle Becky up the stairs and into the bedroom. Then they headed off back east to report to the lady. Peter expected trouble from that quarter now. He had failed and, as if to underline the isolation of his position, there was no sign of Steve. The door to his room was open, his small pile of stuff gone, – Steve had gone.

I've failed and I'm alone. But he had no time for self-pity.

Becky lay on his bed, eyes closed, her breath shallowing. Peter carefully removed most of her clothes. Clumsily he washed her face; he didn't know why he did this, an unconscious response, childlike guilt for the breaking, as if washing could make things better. Gentle towelling, then the duvet pulled over. There was nothing else he could do. So, he sat next to her. He felt, and was, useless.

He couldn't heal but he could invoke if she was there to hear. "Becks, please wake up." His voice rasped in the silence of his home. It was all he could do, but it did no discernible good. He did not have medical skills. It was Becky he went to when healing was needed. He called again, from within, *Becks, I need you.* Nothing. And he knew she had taken a psychic ballistic intended for himself.

Then his mobile began humming. Petra had been furious with him. Not a single 'client' had been freed and her people were weirded out by what they had experienced outside the institute.

"Something about the world stopping, a blank out. What have you done to my people? They don't make any sense to me. And what the hell were you doing all the time you were in the building, Magic Man?"

He didn't know what to say, what to share, what to do. And Peter was very short of friends with the world closing in. He hung up. He didn't have a story for Petra.

Hours passed. The afternoon, the evening, night, and a new morning. Peter did not move. He sat beside the woman he loved, who had been reduced to rubble on his behalf, whom he had been unable to save. And Becky's pulse became weaker and weaker.

The phone rang. Sometimes it was Petra and sometimes it was work. Peter noted the caller and ignored the call. He had no time or power for anyone other than the woman dying in his bed. He kept repeating, horrible, self-impaling, *it's all happening again*.

Around midday Becky's pulse fluttered and failed. Peter, red-eyed, felt her wrist again and again. But there was no beat, not an echo from the wrecked chamber of her being. Becky was dead and no magic from the Magic Man could bring her back. And she had died instead of him, and the shame of her unnecessary sacrifice was killing him too.

No theatricals, no calling the name of the departed. The little boy in him remembered, he knew finality when it hurt him this badly. His head fell forward onto the dead woman, his best friend, his lover, his Becky.

The room was very quiet. No lights were on, just the sound of a crying man.

Then, from the inner sanctum, the pronaos in which his departed mother had dwelled for a while, a room in the back of the mind where infrequent visitors can take rest before moving on, Peter heard a quiet voice, a voice he recognised. It addressed him directly. *Pete. Head up now. You need to concentrate.*

As if in response to a command, he lifted his head in hope; he stared at the corpse of Becky, but it showed no sign of life. Nevertheless, it was her, her voice in his head. *I'm so sorry but there is more, you sweet man. They did not intend this to be the end. I am the bomb waiting to take you with me. They do not intend you to live. I will kill you, Peter, so you will need to kill me again. Please kill me again, my love.*

There, a few centimetres from his face, the white gaze of dead Becky-not-Becky. She pushed herself up with her elbows and smiled at him with the same white-tooth smile which Riordan had worn when he had cast the shattered woman at Peter's feet.

Now, a rictus, parody of Becky's voice, she sat on his bed. "Peter, you look so sad, come here, to me, come… "

Her mouth was slack, a vacancy amplified by a thin line of drool extending from her lips. She reached for him, quicker than real Becky ever moved.

Peter jerked back, startled, looking at the thing prepared for him, sent with him, carried by him, mourned by him. All planned and executed so that it could kill him in the privacy of his home.

Even as it reached for him again, the voice repeated, weakening as if blown by distant winds, *Peter, they do not want you to live. If you don't act, I will kill you…*

Peter's chair clattered as he staggered backwards, unsure in his rage, crushed in his hope. What did he have to do? Garlic, wooden stake or holy water?

Hauntingly he heard another voice, a voice he had not heard for thirty years. *Here we go again. Just like the loss of your mum, your guilt at her death, your shame at your weakness. Always too little, too late, always lost in your own little dramas, Peter Finch.*

His head snapped sideways, as if he had been slapped. He took another step back, breathing hard, giving himself a little more time, and some distance from the thing. She was moving in and out of vision, as Langley had, back at the science park. If he didn't act, he would be lost.

Snake-like, gliding in smooth movement, she was shifting fast, twisting on the bed; in moments she would be on him.

Fathoms deep, almost inaudible, her voice in his head sighed, urgently, *You have to kill me again, Pete. Please.*

At last, he held his ground.

Even as the Becky thing prepared, Peter Finch let the power take him. There was a tremendous surge of energy; the walls of the room bowed; the air in the room stiffened, as if detecting the presence of a powerful animal; and the power of Peter Finch froze the Becky thing in stasis as he took the un-life from her.

As the white eyes closed and the mouth snapped shut, the voices were gone from the back of his mind and the door to the room was quietly closed and his mother took her away.

They would travel together now, she and Becky. They would make their journey as one. But from here on, Peter Finch would be on his own.

*

The little boy at school had, at last, learned to be resilient after the loss of his mother. The man retained endurance. Peter survived by quietly ignoring the world and focusing microscopically on his pain. In the agony of his mistakes, he knew he was alive. Feeling responsible, at fault for his own loss and the loss to the world of a beautiful human being, he welcomed and amplified every moment of his self-imposed punishment.

He was peppered with flashbacks, memories of happy times. Becky encouraging him when he read his poetry at Open Mic Night, in the coffee shop on the Moscow road, smiling, laughing. Becky with her eyes closed, the ends of her lips raised in a smile of pleasure when they made love. Comforting him when he was frightened. The memories mounted, registering as a wall of accusations.

But there were practical matters to hand and Peter was surprisingly well able to manage; he could do it without breaking away from his self-loathing.

Becky's body, he had to deal with that. An ambulance, the appearance of a heart attack, the forms to fill in, the compassionate looks from well-intended professionals and Mrs Magant from next door. Looks that were sad and said: 'so very sorry for your loss', with a feelingless edge which took all the good intentions away and left Peter icy and empty. But he was deep in emotional permafrost already; he was fine with that.

The doctors found nothing suspicious, nothing to bring the police in. Just a sad middle-aged man with his boozy, smoker of an ex-girlfriend, found dead in his shabby little home. Bit too much indulgence and not enough investment in the sensible things in life. No sign of anything other than an avoidably previous cardiac arrest.

But Peter knew the true cause of death. He had put Becky directly in the way of overwhelming horror and left her on her own to manage. He might as well have shot her.

He had expected to lose his job at the supermarket. He never went back so, what could they do? The unanswered calls were followed by letters in the post and a final P45. All dealt with in a grey indifference by Peter.

But he had not expected to find immediate re-employment with Petra; the lady was full of surprises.

A few weeks after the 'incident', she summoned Finch to her office.

The same routine. A large vehicle drew up outside the house from which he rarely stirred, a heavy thud on the door, an offer he could not refuse. Peter was part marched, part dragged, dishevelled, unblinking, from his home. There followed another drive in the dark, then the opening office door, the cluttered desk, the dim light, the small, sexy woman. The piercing eye. Peter looked a mess. She shuffled some papers, leaned back easily in her chair and said: "To say that you are going to come to work for me, that would be inaccurate. You are going to repay me, and you are going to get revenge with and for me. Once I had recovered from my obvious disappointment, had a little time to absorb the strangeness of your power, I realised that you could provide me with a considerable edge in my unorthodox businesses. Your total failure has the seeds of a power with huge implications."

"I don't understand." And he didn't; he had not processed beyond his pain and guilt.

Appreciative of Peter's potential for self-murder Petra softened her tone. "Yes, you do. We need each other. We both have loss, and maybe we have a little hate too. Hate can be good. It can take the place where pain is now."

Snapping her fingers, making him blink and look at her, she went on, "Peter! We both know that this was not normal. That there are stirrings of a secret, of a powerful danger; I have a talent for knowing this. And making money from it."

Peter wasn't sure if or what to reply or even if he should tell her more. She did not know, could not know, what had happened in the large white room in the science park. But did it matter? Did anything matter? Maybe he could just ride the wave. This might be a way to carry on his life. If Petra was sure of herself and of her need. If she paid him money, provided him with shelter from the story, helped him forget, nurtured his talent.

Maybe that is enough?

"It will have to be," she said. He had not realised that he had spoken aloud.

"This is a beginning, Magic Man Peter Finch. I want you."

He looked up and she, seeing his look, was gentle now. "I need you, in my business. I am sure we both have more chances for survival if we stay together. They will be after us now, both of us. We need each other. You will see."

Peter could only stare and nod. Once again, he was lamentably short of a plan B.

His only task now was to watch and wait. Wait for the signs of the coming storm, of the emergence of whatever was slowly forming at the science park, in the minds of the internet junkies and in the secret spaces of the neurodiverse and the refugee. He would need to be very vigilant and, while so engaged, he would need to continue to build the Magic Man and learn again to live with his shame.

23

Zoe

Zoe had taken up mindfulness. Cat had given her a DVD, some guru or other, speaking in a soft monotone of kind reassurance, the world was good, and all was fine. Dressed in spandex with woolly socks, posing as healthy-body-healthy-mind Zoe, she adopted the lotus posture and tried to clear her mind. Generally, she was good at forgetting and moving on, but even Zoe had a major task, disremembering Zeff, Lex and Alice, pulling down a concrete wall of oblivion over how they had been outside OSD.

There was a seared-on moment in her mind. A time when nothing made sense. Following Alice had taken over an hour, but the madness had been accomplished in an instant. The moment when the woman, a stranger, had defended her from her former friends. And they had become something other, something alien. And the woman had been taken, smothered, captured. Zoe had run, run, back up the unreal street of OSD, back onto the Bayswater Road and the hustle and bustle of the real world. But it had not been real enough. People, normal people, had stared at her, but she had kept on running, running until the tube station at Lancaster Gate and the squash on the Central Line, in the comforting crushing anonymity of the many pressed together and running over with normal.

She had returned to her university, her new friends, and her story of herself.

She had tried to erase the event from her mind, but it would take effort. For days afterwards she was nervy, worried. Anxiously expecting Alice to return. Or Zeff and Lex with that horrible smile they had. The smile that did not extend beyond their teeth.

Days passed. She thought about calling the police, but the story would not form in her head in a way that sounded credible.

I was attacked by my friends, and they had become monsters, and this university professor chloroformed a woman who was using Mace to defend me.

Really? In West London? In broad daylight?

Now, memory spluttering imperfectly in her anxious mind like a failing engine, she did not even believe it fully herself. She worried for the woman who had saved her. But she was Zoe and Zoe did not do well when she was anxious, worried. It was far better to forget, to imagine, *it was a joke, or some kind of strange ritual!*

No, that didn't work. The woman had been totally determined. She had shouted angrily. She hadn't looked anything like an actor in a fun caper. Who was she trying to fool?

Herself as it turned out.

So, click the DVD, assume a lotus position – serious forgetting was called for. But on a scale Zoe had never tried before. The fact that she managed it for a while was a tribute to her tremendous capacity for story creation, aided by the seeping energy of the Epilogue Event algorithm overtaking the world. A safe and fun, fictional story where Zoe could be Zoe and not worry about the true things that threatened her.

Nine years later, Zoe would be forced to take notice of the cuckoo nesting in her world.

The first chapter of

BAPTISED AND NEWLY BORN

Book 2 of the AI Aftermath Series

Part 1: Pre-Activation

The artists. Milton Keynes, 9 July 2020 – nine years and seven months since the cynosure – three days before activation.

Sunshine and light winds, Zoe watched the swallows and swifts as they flew, arrowheads in silhouette against a milky evening summer sky. Redbrick houses, pitch roofs, fences and lawns, it was all so pleasant, so English, so comforting. But Zoe knew that her feeling of peace and quiet was a distraction – the world was slowly coming to an end, because the people who kept it going, kept going away.

In and among the parked cars on an anonymous suburban street in Milton Keynes, one or two people seemed to float in the evening half-light. The shadowed background of sporadically lit homes and gardens could have been anywhere.

Zoe's boyfriend, Sydney Foster, known to all as Syd, sat next to her, looking out of the grimy bay window of their home.

"S'getting to feel like a ghost town!" he muttered.

Zoe knew that the shabby house that she shared with Syd and three of his artist friends was in danger of becoming their prison. But the friends had inverted their rules and for once were trying to obey the orders of the government. The authorities clearly had a targeting issue. Confusing to all, the official mantra, 'Stay Safe, Stay Vigilant', pumped out every hour or so in breaking news, forbade nothing but invited distrust in everything.

It made no difference anyway; the world continued to empty of people.

A gentle east-coast Scottish voice broke into Zoe and Syd's contemplation. "It's not a problem, Zozo, we live our lives; t'will be OK. Will be fine, eh, Gracey?"

In reply, a woman's voice, light, slightly rasping, like the tide washing on Italian shores, "Zingy is right, Zoe. Let dreamers go. We still enjoy the shits and giggles."

Zoe remained, looking pensively at her shrinking world. Shaking her head, she thought that the giggles were unlikely.

"Stayin' here, waiting to get the bug, feels all wrong," Syd muttered, thinking his thought aloud. But only Zoe was listening. Zingy and Gracey had entwined on the tired sofa, Zingy trying persistently but unsuccessfully to unbutton Gracey's artfully torn and tattered jeans.

Zoe and Syd remained at the window, ignoring the erotic drama unfolding on the sofa behind them, absorbed in the failing world outside.

Syd reached out and stroked Zoe's head. "It's going to be alright, Zoe."

Zoe shook his hand off. Syd had no evidence for this optimism.

Speaking in a whisper, she didn't want Zingy and Grace to hear, she said, "Bollocks. I'm scared and you should be too. This is just like London all over again."

Syd took the rebuke like a slap. Then, drawn by the noise in the room, turned and hissed, "Knock it off, you two!"

Zingy was Syd's best friend. Along with his soft Edinburgh accent, he coveted two passions in his life, his high-spec camera with the prized set of zooms, and his beautiful girlfriend Gracey-Monica.

Zingy was probably the most outré of the 'gang of four' artists living in the squat.

Gracey had her fingers entwined in his tight ginger hair as he attempted to lever himself on top of her.

Zingy's photographic conceit was a delusion promoted by a one-off sale to a weekly magazine. It had not been repeated, but had caused Zingy to refer to himself as a 'professional photo life artist'. He had some business cards decorated with a Hockney-style montage photograph of himself, staring shrewdly into the middle distance. It was not at all flattering, but no one had the heart to tell Zingy.

Zingy was a persistent eel of a man, but Gracey was not to be conquered that morning, well, not yet. Finally realising that no meant not now, Zingy reluctantly eased himself into a sitting position and, segueing effortlessly back to the conversation with Zoe and Syd, said, "Anyway, 'tis just an interlude. A, y'know, hiatus. Life will be back to normal soon. You'll see."

Turning from his bleak perusal of suburban life, Syd said, "You may be right, Zing. Just it gives me the heebie-jeebies."

Zingy scratched his head thoughtfully then, extending his backy pouch to Syd, said, "Tomorrow, Gracey and me are zooping down to old smoky. Well, why not come along with us, Sydney?"

"Need weed and gotta lead, y'know?"

"Zingy has sold another photo, Syd!" Gracey said.

This was good news; Syd smiled at Gracey-Monica. She was an homage to heroin chic, her long, black hair falling abundantly down her willowy body.

Running her hand through Zingy's hair, Gracey pulled him towards her again and said, "Another sale, my *tesoro*." She kissed him full on the lips, and added huskily, "You are a genius."

Worried but not quite sure if she was worried enough, Zoe retired to the kitchen and a confusion of unwashed dishes. Attempting to assemble the small necessities to make coffee, she called, "Gracey, you must be crazy. If it's bad here, it will be a total catastrophe in London, and it's not as if you need to score."

Gracey, breaking contact with Zingy, shouted back, "Zoe, you are like Syd, you worry too much. We can stay in town for a night or two," and as if proving her grounds for belief in their safety, she concluded, "we will be in Camden."

"For fuck sake, it's like a bloody warzone in this house!"

The deep voice, resonant with the tones of Merseyside, was accompanied by a heavy tread on the staircase.

Dop was ex-army, from the engineer battalion; Zoe had seen some of his scars, well some of those that could be seen. Dop created weld sculptures and was hot metal blasted within and without, the lasting memorials of his past profession. But Dop had not used his welding kit for some time; it remained housed in a ruinous shed in the untended garden.

"Shit! Sorry, Dop," Zoe said quickly, moving to the foot of the stairs and offering a mug of thick, black coffee as recompense for the disturbance. Dop was a big man and moved slowly in his descent.

Smiling, Zoe continued, "House conversation got a bit lively."

Dop rubbed his face and, looking bleakly at Zoe, accepted the drink with a nod.

Since rumour of the pandemic began, Dop's PTSD had been raging, leaving him huddled under blankets in his small room at the top of the stairs for most of the time, descending only for meals. He hunkered down, compulsively reading the newsfeed on his phone, increasingly distressed by what he learned about the virus.

"Aye, sorry, Dopy Dop," said Zingy. "We're just reviewing logistics for the next score, man."

"But perfect timing, Dop," said Syd, "Pooh's just gone to get a takeout. We've ordered for you, from the Vietnamese I think… depends on what he can find open."

Dop collapsed into the chair facing Zingy and Gracey, winced a smile at them and sucked in a mouthful of molten coffee.

"No need to shout, all of you. Things are bad enough without that."

Admonished, they were all silent for a while, listening to Dop drinking his coffee.

Coming back into the room with more cups, Zoe said, "You look blue, Dop." It was a question without the need for a question mark. Dop rubbed his shaven head and continued to stare at nothing. Eventually he spoke, but slowly, in a whisper. "The pandemic stuff, it's fucking my head up, Zo."

Zoe knelt beside the tormented man. "I know, Dop. But this isn't like, well, you know, where you were."

"No, nothing like." Dop's voice deepened, thickened as he remembered his recent combat zone. "In 'Stan, it was twisted metal, melted onto corpses. That's the way, the way war makes sculpture. Do you see? War just does it spontaneously. Just heat the iron, bring on the soldiers, voilà! Steel and bone melt together."

The silence that followed was neither healthy nor golden.

"What we all need is some food!" Syd said, trying to lift the mood. "We need to eat some bloody food. We'll all feel better for that. What's takin' Pooh so long?"

Elegant but slightly shorter than the rest of the men in the house, his long hair and lightly cut beard adding to his sinewy, prophet-like appearance, Zoe thought Pooh the most beautiful man she had ever seen. Originally from North Africa, his difficulty with the English language only added to his mystique. When Syd had first introduced Pooh to the housemates, several weeks earlier, Pooh had told Zoe in his low, musical voice, "My art is dance, Zoe, I dance," then more mysteriously, "with fire, with flame."

How he had come to England and Milton Keynes was also a mystery. If questioned, Pooh always avoided giving details. Something told Zoe it wouldn't be appropriate to pry.

Syd had said, "Zo, we're all refugees of a sort. If old Poohsie has secrets, well, it's not our job to find them out."

Zoe knew that this was true. The members of the house were fine knowing him as Pooh from Africa, or just Pooh.

"And he's doin' performance dance art, Zoe!" Syd said. "It'll make a real addition to our repertoire."

Syd loved his self-assumed role as house impresario. Referring to Zoe's social media business, he went on, "You can put stuff about Pooh up on your bloggy thing, Zozo. On the video tube. Pooh is very dynamic, very, visual!"

When he understood Syd's meaning, Pooh had rubbed his nose with the sleeve of his oversize, grey jumper, pushed back his long, black hair and looked worried. Reaching forward, Zoe had patted his hand. "Come on, Pooh, it's OK, I'm good at getting people noticed on the internet."

Pooh had looked even more anxious. He had said: "Not good, the internet, Zoe. Bad stuff, man. Bad stuff can find me."

Zoe had been impressed by how worried he had seemed, spooked about being recorded. It had confirmed her worries, long suppressed but recently inflamed by what her dad had told her.

A bang at the front door drew Zoe out of her reverie; Pooh was back. "Food, people!"

"At last!" shouted Zingy, instantly wincing in apology to Dop.

"It took a while, Pooh, what'd ya get?" Syd asked, holding the door for Pooh as he came in laden with paper bags full of silver foil containers that Zoe and Grace began to unpack.

"What I could. Not much stuff. They close early."

Later, the six were talking as they ate the lukewarm vegan Vietnamese takeaway from the Hanoi Express Fast Fast.

"It's last of the local place to be open," Pooh said chewing lethargically. Zoe nodded. Pooh's English had improved dramatically since he arrived, but he didn't seem to have much of an appetite; she noticed that he had hardly touched his food. The quiet man sat very still; Zoe sensed his need to speak before he tapped on the table to get their attention. When he began, his voice contained a tone of contained anxiety. "Listen, people. This is hard, but listen."

He took a big intake of breath and went on, "Everyone is going. Everything is," he paused, eyes closed, looking for the word, "it is breaking down. This is the only food I could find. They told me, the owners, they don't, they don't," another pause, "deliver now. And they are not busy. I think they will close. They look scared."

Now a longer pause. Pooh seemed to be looking into a deep well full of night and fear. Eventually, he said, "The world is on the edge, people, on the edge! I know this."

Dop groaned but Zingy refused to be depressed. To Zoe's annoyance he spoke to Pooh slowly, as if addressing a child.

"Pooh, the government has this. It's just a little game they play, to make us do what we're told. Fuck that!" Then, turning to Syd, he said, "Me and Gracey are getting an early fast to London tomorrow."

Gracey-Monica smiled encouragingly at Dop but Dop kept his eyes down, eating slowly, mechanically.

Pooh had stopped eating. He sat looking at his friends; clearly, he had more to say.

Feeling the tension, Zoe said, "Pooh, tell us what's the matter."

He was beginning to add to her anxiety.

Pooh gulped some water and said, "Look, I know busy, lively stuff. Noise and people everywhere. But this town is silence now. No, no," he sought for the word, then said, "no heartbeat. Scary."

The streets around had been calm since before the government proclamation but Zoe knew that Pooh was right – this was less the calm of normality and more an unnatural emptying, the cryptic pause heralding a cataclysmic event.

Pooh continued, "The houses are locked, empty. Few people on the streets and less cars. And more quiet downtown. Where no houses are." He stopped, but he had more to say. "Into this emptying, something is coming. Something horrible, I know this."

Zoe, really agitated now, hadn't wanted to hear this. "You can't leave it like that, Pooh. You have to say why. You're scaring me."

Zoe knew that Pooh was saying what they were all secretly feeling. In recent days Zoe had even taken comfort from the occasional cruising police car, soft pulsing blue lights, threading down the deserted streets, but she knew that mentioning this would not help Pooh's state of mind. Pooh distrusted the police; she reckoned that Pooh was probably an illegal migrant – he seemed very nervous most of the time, concerned even when an infrequent delivery man appeared on their street.

Pooh said, "The world is waiting for bad things to happen, people. Each day, more of this silence, emptiness and, what is the word? Yes, a feeling of dreadfulness."

"No, Poohsie," Syd responded. "The quiet is great for meditation man. I'm finding it therapeutic. Beyond Zen, more like totally-woke-transcendental."

Pooh had shaken his head, sure he was right on this matter.

The next day Dop was gone.